GW00992132

About the author

Kerrin Doward was born and raised in Bath and started her career as a police officer and detective, but the majority of her working life was as a dog trainer and behaviourist which has come in very handy as she has owned a total of six very active and mischievous Irish Setters. Kerrin has had numerous articles published in national magazines helping other dog trainers and owners, but having now moved to Cornwall with her wife and very spoiled dog, Aggi, she is focussing on writing spine tingling horrors and thought-provoking mysteries for the middle grade and young adult reader.

As well as having a love of dogs and all nature, Kerrin has a keen interest in magic and mysticism.

This is a work of fiction. Names, characters, businesses, places, events and incidents are either the products of the author's imagination or used in a fictitious manner. Any resemblance to actual persons, living or dead, or actual events is purely coincidental.

ABANDON ALL HOPE

KERRIN DOWARD

ABANDON ALL HOPE

Vanguard Press

VANGUARD PAPERBACK

© Copyright 2022
Kerrin Doward

The right of Kerrin Doward to be identified as author of
this work has been asserted by her in accordance with the
Copyright, Designs and Patents Act 1988.

All Rights Reserved

No reproduction, copy or transmission of this publication
may be made without written permission.
No paragraph of this publication may be reproduced,
copied or transmitted save with the written permission of the
publisher, or in accordance with the provisions
of the Copyright Act 1956 (as amended).

Any person who commits any unauthorised act in relation to
this publication may be liable to criminal
prosecution and civil claims for damages.

A CIP catalogue record for this title is
available from the British Library.

ISBN 978 1 80016 501 4

Vanguard Press is an imprint of
Pegasus Elliot Mackenzie Publishers Ltd.
www.pegasuspublishers.com

First Published in 2022

Vanguard Press
Sheraton House Castle Park
Cambridge England

Printed & Bound in Great Britain

Dedication

For my wife, Cassie, and my dog, Aggi, who both hid
under the bedclothes when I read this to them

Acknowledgements

My thanks go firstly to my wife, Cassie, who has been subjected to tirelessly reading and re-reading this book numerous times. To my dog, Aggi, for laying patiently by my side whilst I write and to my brother, David, whose propensity for unusual accidents as a child, brought memories to the fore.

Chapter One

"Occultism! Devil worship! Witchcraft! Or just coincidence and bad luck! Call it what you will. The fact is that many visitors to that old cottage in the hills were reported to have died highly suspicious and agonising deaths." Mr Marchant sits on his desk facing the class, his legs swinging casually as he scratches his neatly trimmed dark beard and ruffles his wavy brown hair.

Despite his six years of experience as a teacher, having finally got the undivided attention of the whole class for once, he then totally misjudges his audience by warning them of the dangers of the open mineshafts and the legends of the Cornish knockers, spriggans and other fae folk who inhabit the moorland. The class not only stop listening but soon start to look vacantly anywhere other than at him.

Hearing his voice echoing emptily back to him, he continues weakly, "Of course, it is also reported that if you should be on the moor after dark, you need to watch out, for the Devil riding a big black horse is sure to chase you down." Mr Marchant looks expectantly at the fourteen and fifteen-year-olds in Year 10 but sees that the shocked response he had hoped for isn't going to be forthcoming. Wanting to get his message across but seeing nothing but blank, disinterested faces, he is forced to revert back to his original tale, the only one that seems to have grabbed the attention of such sceptical teenagers: the more Devilish, evil aspects of the legends surrounding the moor. He is going to have to lay it on thick to get them listening again, so looks directly at Jack, the popular, uber cool, surf dude of the class. If he could at least persuade Jack to not go on the moor over the summer holidays, then the rest of the class are likely to follow suit.

Quickly he adds, "And, for the more cynically minded amongst you who don't believe in the likes of faeries and goblins, it is well worth taking note that in that derelict and now haunted cottage, sitting amongst those rugged, wild hills, lived a real-life Satanist." This time his legs stop swinging and he sits very still, his eyes wide open, as he pauses for effect before continuing. "Some say, he was possessed by the Devil. Some say he *was* the Devil!"

Eyes that had been focussed on not very well-hidden mobile phones under desks or gazing dreamily out of the window turn directly towards him. Boom! he's got them back in the palm of his hand. He feels like punching the air but instead he nods gravely.

"He was a real person, you know. He held séances and black masses where he purportedly summoned not only the dead but also demonic beasts."

Twenty-two sets of eyebrows raise simultaneously.

He pushes on. "His black magic rituals and Satanic rites resulted in some of his guests losing their lives in the most gruesome of ways." Mr Marchant is satisfied. He seems to have got not only Jack's undivided attention but that of the whole class.

During the summer every year he hears reports of the Coastguard being called out to both adults and children who on a nice, warm sunny day have gone exploring on the moor only to get lost amongst the heavy mist that unexpectedly, and swiftly, rolls in from the sea. Many go missing overnight, lost amongst the harsh, dark landscape of granite rocks, gorse and heather, and are not found until the next day, shivering from both the cold and fear. Many more are hospitalised due to hypothermia or broken bones, having stumbled on the rocky ground in the dark or fallen from great heights. Occasionally some meet a far, far worse ending. Hopefully, this year, his tales of local folklore and legend, as the final lesson of term, will put them all off climbing up there.

The bell rings and grabbing their jackets, bags and anything left on their desks, the class scramble to be out of school for the long-awaited summer holidays as quickly as possible. In a rush for the door, they call their goodbyes,

"Cheers, Mr M."

"Have a good one, sir."

"See ya…"

But Mr Marchant replies before Jack has time to complete his sentence. "Yeah, yeah, Jack, I know, don't wanna be ya." and laughs, waving Jack away. Mr Marchant can easily remember patiently watching the large, old fashioned, white plastic framed circular clock on the wall behind the teacher's desk when he had been at school. It was always two minutes slow so when the black hands hit 3:31 p.m. he knew the freedom bell, as he used to think of it, was coming at any moment. After all, he is still only thirteen years older than Year 10 himself.

Walking out of school Tom, the class techie, throws his blazer over his shoulder and pushes his black framed glasses further up his nose with his index finger, something he does regularly. No one knows whether it's because the frames are too loose, or it has just become a habit. Tom is what a grandmother would call good-looking in a 'clean cut way'.

"He must think we're all kids to believe that stuff," he says with a note of sarcasm in his voice.

Jack laughs, replying, "He's just doing his best to stop anyone from going onto the moors over the summer holidays. Ehh-ehh." He makes a sound like a wrong answer buzzer, adding, "Big fail, 'cause as it just so happens, it's more likely to *encourage* us to go."

Lewis, their Scottish, ginger haired mate, six month's Tom and Jack's junior, stops suddenly, holding both his hands out questioningly in front of him. "Hey, we've got a whole six weeks off so why don't we?"

They look at him. "Why don't we go up onto the moor to see if we can find the sprinkles and get chased by the Devil on horseback?" he laughs.

"They're called spriggans," Tom corrects him, adding scornfully, "They're not real; they're just something parents tell small kids about to make them behave."

"Yeah! Or to keep tourists away," Jack adds, laughing.

"Okay! Okay! Well, we can give the sprinkles or spriggans, or whatever they're called, a swerve, but we really should go and look for the so-called, haunted cottage. You've got to admit that sounds pretty interesting." Lewis had obviously been paying more attention to all of Mr Marchant's tales than his appearance in class had let on and sounds keen to go exploring. Poor Mr Marchant; his cautionary tales and words of warning had unfortunately had completely the opposite effect.

"Yeah, it'll be something to do, I guess." Jack replies distractedly. He doesn't want to show that he is just as keen as Lewis to go exploring as he's got his cool reputation to think of, but he has also just spotted his girlfriend waiting for him.

Amelie is leaning against the gate, long tanned legs reaching out from the bottom of her slightly shorter than the school prescribed length skirt allowed. Everyone at school, teachers, boys and girls alike, can't fail to recognise what a stunningly beautiful girl she is. She has already changed her shoes and is standing with one stacked floral Van crossed over the other, absent-mindedly stroking her long blonde hair into a flowing stream of the palest gold over one shoulder towards her waist. Tom and Lewis, also looking across at the two girls, grin at each other and raise their eyebrows knowingly, indicating that they believe this is where Jack seems to have recently picked up a similar habit of playing with his hair from. Amelie's perfect white teeth and ice blue eyes sparkle as she throws her head back and laughs at something Mia is saying to her. Even her laugh has a tinkling crystal sound to it.

Amelie doesn't attract Tom's attention for long, however, as Tom only has eyes for Mia. He is totally and utterly entranced by the girl whose grey and green flecked hazel eyes flash through her tortoise shell framed glasses when she is explaining something to him and whose chin length dark bob further adds to her somewhat serious and intellectual appearance. She reminds him a bit of Velma, the girl in the old Scooby Doo films. Mia is the sensible one; the one who knows pretty much everything, the one who would be able to work a way out of any given situation. As soon as Mia speaks, Tom can't help but focus on her small, red lipped mouth, losing himself in whatever words are forthcoming. He hasn't ever even noticed her invisible aligners, which is just as well seeing as how much her parents had had to pay for them instead of braces. Mia is brilliantly clever, especially at maths and that, in itself, is hugely attractive to Tom.

Lewis, however, is not in the least bit interested in having a girlfriend. There are enough annoying females at home, and he knows only too well how high maintenance they can be. His sisters hog the only bathroom, spending ages soaking themselves in poncey smelling bath bombs or leaving tangles of long hair in the shower plug, that seem to attract grey waxy goo when you try to pull them out. The bathroom cabinets are bursting with sponges to put make up on, cotton wool to take it off again, moisturisers for day and different ones for night, and they are only thirteen and sixteen-years-old, for goodness' sake. Then of course there's the tears. They cry at sad films. They cry at films with happy endings. You just can't win. And that's not to mention the talking. Geez! They sure can do a *lot* of talking. Anyway, there's only one person worth really bothering spending time with, Lewis has already decided.

Reaching the entrance, Jack possessively kisses Amelie on the cheek, slides his arm around her waist, turning her around in one swift movement as they walk out of school; Two on fleek, tanned, blonde, beach-beautiful people. A few steps behind them Tom and Mia are already deep in conversation about something cerebral and bringing up the rear is Lewis, smiling to himself, grateful that he doesn't have to put up with all this demanding girlfriend stuff but happy to be on the periphery with his friends.

They have six weeks of summer holidays ahead of them so despite it only being three-fifty in the afternoon, his stomach already rumbling, Jack wants to get home for something to eat. Grabbing Amelie, he pulls her to him, and whopping a lip lock straight on to her smacker, says, "Laters, babe!"

Throwing her hair over one shoulder she pouts at him and looks expectantly at Mia who says her goodbyes to Tom as formally as if they had only just been introduced. Jack laughs inwardly. He always expects them to shake hands. The girls, walking side by side and immediately engrossed in conversation once again, stride away.

"Coming?" Jack asks Tom and Lewis.

"No can do today," Tom says, eager to head home to start his research surrounding the cottage on the moor.

Lewis raises his eyebrows "Nor me. Family end of school barbeque this evening," he says, having just that second decided that if Tom isn't going back to Jack's, he may as well head home early and help set everything up.

"Oh, okay! Let's meet up at mine tomorrow then, huh? We can make a plan about going up to have a root around that cottage. See what it's all about, yeah?" Jack suggests, remembering the conversation they had been having before meeting up with the girls. The three agree a time and at the roundabout, they all set off in different directions towards home.

Chapter Two

Tom turns into Woodhedge End, a pretty tree lined avenue where he and his family live in a tall, three-storied semi-detached Georgian style house fronted by a large hedge of bay. It is a beautiful house, painted white with large sash windows and five steps up to a front door that sports a large black metal hooped door knocker. His mother's funky little green and white Mini Cooper and his father's sleek silver Audi A5 are both absent from the gravelled double driveway, indicating that they are still at work. Both his parents work long hours and Tom knows they won't be home for at least three or more hours yet, so he'll have to wait until much later for his dinner.

He hangs his blazer and bag on the row of coat hooks in the long hallway and neatly places his shoes in the rack beneath. Smelling the aroma of warm toast coming from the direction of the kitchen, he pads his way in his socks over the red and black tiled floor. His sister, Kate, the eldest of the three children is sitting at the breakfast bar, absent-mindedly curling a strand of her long dark hair around one finger as she leans over a magazine, dreamily nibbling on the browned bread; melted butter dripping off onto her knee.

"Hey," she calls without even looking round.

"Hey," Tom replies, making a bee line for the loaf, slicing a chunk off, and popping it straight into the toaster. Mr Marchant's lesson still on his mind, he asks "Do you know anything about an old, haunted cottage on the moor?"

"Moor?" She isn't really listening.

"Yes, an old cottage on top of the moor where black magic took place, do you know anything about it?" he adds.

"Only that people that visit it go blind and die horrible deaths, screaming in agony."

Just what Tom wanted to hear. "Really? Wow!" He is fascinated.

"That's what I've heard anyway." Kate doesn't want to engage in further conversation, and sticking her nose back in her story about the adventures of two young backpackers in Australia, she ignores any further questions from Tom. Tom takes his toast upstairs to his bedroom, passing the open door of Sophie's bedroom. Sophie, two years older than him and one year younger than Kate, is lazing on the bed, still in her school uniform, hands behind her head, listening to music with her earbuds in. Tom can just about hear the underlying beat of *doof tch tch tch,* meaning Sophie must, as usual, be playing the music very loudly. Tom thinks Sophie was born thirty years too late with her passion for drum and bass music.

She yells out over the top, the family standard greeting, "Hey."

"Hey," Tom replies and waves, knowing that there is no point in saying more as Sophie can't possibly hear him. In his room, Tom doesn't even stop to change out of his uniform, but sits down at his desk, switches on his PC, munching on his toast whilst waiting for it to load. He types into the search bar. Satisfied with the first headline that flashes up on his screen 'Thrill Seekers Photograph Abandoned House Of The Dark Arts', Tom calls out, "Yes!" to no one.

***

All the terraced houses in Jack's street, look pretty much the same, except his. It is always easy for people to find Jack's house with its bright yellow painted window frames and door. A low stone wall surrounds the little garden at the front that consists of an eight-foot square of concrete, a rainbow painted wooden bench, terracotta pots of flowers and a cherry tree with metal wind chimes and small, glinting mirrors hanging on multi-coloured ribbons to catch the sun. 'It is a sunny, happy looking house even just from the outside,' thinks Jack, catching sight of it as he turns the corner. He opens the front door, pushes his way through a multicoloured bead curtain and walks along the hall, its walls covered by numerous paintings of strange shapes and bold colours.

"Is that you, Jack? I'm in the studio!" his mother quickly calls.

Jack walks through the house and into the courtyard at the back of the house where his mother has converted what had once been nothing more than a brick shed, into a bright and airy space with good light, just right for an abstract artist. She turns towards him, holding a plastic kitchen spatula covered in red paint in one hand, a paint brush stuck in the mop of blonde hair she has loosely tied on top of her head, and spits out another brush that she was holding between her teeth. "Hi, sweetie. How was your last day?"

"Yeah, okay," Jack replies.

"No Tom or Lewis today?" she asks, looking past Jack. The two friends go back to Jack's so often after school for tea and cake that Mrs Dory has allocated each of them their own gold rimmed, multi-coloured, flowered, un-matching teacup and saucer, more befitting of a group of nanas out for afternoon tea at the vicarage.

"Nah, busy today," Jack explains.

"All the more for us then," his mother grins.

At just about the same time as Tom is asking his sister a similar question, Jack asks his mum, "Have you heard about the cottage on the moor? Supposed to have had some evil guy living there and people dying and stuff."

"Well, yes, I've heard the rumours, but it was a very long time ago, and I don't think anyone lives there now." She shakes her head, adding, "Why do you ask?"

"Oh, just that Mr M was telling us about it today. We think he was trying to spook us to keep us away but it just kinda sounds interesting, you know?"

Jack's mum does know. Her mind momentarily wanders off to seventeen years ago when she had first met Jack's father whilst picnicking, with a friend, under the tall granite rocks that overlooked the cottage. They had been too interested in each other to bother trudging their way across the overgrown garden but her friend, deciding to give them a bit of space, had wandered off but gone no further than the back door. She had told Jack's mum that there was an eerie feeling about the place that gave her goosepimples and she had heard noises from inside and been too frightened to enter alone. Unlike her friend, who was as white as a sheet when she returned and refused to go back, Jack's mum had always intended to visit the cottage but had never got around to it.

Smiling she suddenly jumps up saying brightly, "Right you, I'm guessing you're starving as always."

Jack knows the drill. He hangs his blazer on the back door handle and sits down at the white painted table with its four wooden chairs, each painted a different colour. He watches his mother making tea and cutting two generous slices of lemon drizzle cake, ready for their catch up on the events of each other's day. Jack always enjoys this time with his mum. She never fails to be there when he gets home and is always interested in what he has done. So, animatedly, he regales almost the entire content of Mr Marchant's lesson on local legends and the Satanist who had lived high up on the moor. Another student who, despite his apparent lack of interest, had obviously been listening all along.

***

Lewis has much further to walk home as he lives on a large smallholding, more like a small farm, on the outskirts of town. It is a very loud and busy household as there are eight of them in the house: his parents, his mother's parents, his younger sister, elder sister and his elder brother. All four of the children have the tightly curled ginger hair of their mother and their grandmother. Lewis loves living as part of a large family; there is always someone around and always some drama or excitement to get involved in, even if it is just one of the numerous family arguments that happen living this close together, but he feels safe and comfortable knowing that underneath it all there is also a lot of laughter and a lot of love. As well as the human occupants of the smallholding there are sheep, chickens, goats, Mabel a Vietnamese pot-bellied pig, Rusty and Tinker the Jack Russell dogs, or the Jack Rats, as Lewis refers to them. There are also ducks, two geese, Jemima and Gertrude; his younger sister's guinea pigs and Misty the grey cat. Strictly speaking Misty isn't really their cat; she just wandered into the large farmhouse style kitchen one day bringing a present of a dead mouse and has stayed ever since.

It's a very hot, sunny day as Lewis trudges up the dusty track that leads from the lane up to the farmhouse. He is forced to pick a side and walk along one of the ruts because of the long grass growing down the middle where the tractor and car wheels miss it. He is trying to decide whether to get the ride-on mower out before the barbeque or leave it until the next day, when just as he hears feet running up behind him, he receives a hard slap on the back, the familiar greeting of Matt, his older brother.

"Good day at school?" Matt asks.

"Guess so. All the better for being the last one of term," Lewis laughs, adding, "What do you know about the haunted cottage on the moor?"

"The evil place with the demonic beast that roams at night taking the souls of all who visit?" Matt asks, looking at Lewis with a pretend scared face.

"You know it? Have you been there?" Lewis is excited.

"Yeah, of course," Matt lies, adding, "Reeeeeally scary. Lots of weird stuff went down there. People were found writhing on the floor in agony, with blood coming out of their eyes and everything!" Matt has never been there at all, but he has heard the rumours associated with the cottage and the intrigue surrounding its infamous occupant. Walking up the rutted track, the central strip of long grass between them, Lewis listens intently to Matt's made-up tales of how he stayed the night despite hearing howling outside and how his belongings had risen-up into the air and been flung around the room by a poltergeist. He admires his eldest brother, and believing every word that Matt tells him, he wants to show him that he too can be brave, so determines there and then that not only will he, Tom and Jack visit the haunted cottage, but he will persuade them that they should stay overnight too.

Chapter Three

At just before eleven the next morning, Lewis catches up with Tom as he turns the corner into Jack's street. The familiar, cheery sound of the windchimes gently tinkle before the house even comes into view. The door is opened by Jack's mum.

"Morning, Mrs Dory," Tom greets her.

"Morning, gentlemen. Jack's up in his room," she replies, pointing up the stairs.

"Dory! Jack Dory!" Lewis laughs. He still finds it funny every time he hears it spoken aloud. Although Jack is his given name, Lewis's grandad had told him that back in the old days, Jack used to be a nickname for people called John. Fancy a dude who spends half his life in the water being called John Dory, like the fish.

Tom just bats his eyes at Lewis. "Yeah, it's only four years you've been hearing that," he says, unamused and taking them two at a time, he bounces up the stairs, with Lewis following close behind.

Jack is sitting on his bed, a laptop on his knees, playing a noisy computer game and is concentrating so hard he doesn't appear to notice them come in; if he does, he certainly doesn't bother to show it.

Lewis thinks how cool Jack's bedroom is with a full-sized surfboard leaning against the corner of the wall; giant posters of surfers riding the tube and fabulous underwater shots looking up at waves as they break.

Tom, however, looks at the curtains of many colours; the clothes strewn across the floor, the back of a wicker seat and on the duvet that shows a mandala with a multicoloured elephant, and thinks it is all way too busy for his taste. He likes his bedroom to be tidy and orderly with his books stacked alphabetically in his bookcase, his first aid kit immediately to hand, his PC placed centrally on his desk beneath his window and his bedding and curtains to match the plain magnolia and white colour theme.

Lewis, on the other hand, had his room painted blue before he was even born, and since his parents consider blue a suitable colour for a boy, it hasn't been decorated since. He thinks about how ironic it is really that blue is the favoured bedroom colour when they seemed to have dressed him in nothing but green or rust colours all his life; apparently, they suit his ginger hair and pale freckled complexion. Nevertheless, that is the colour he is still stuck with: blue walls, blue curtains, blue bedding, and no picture posting allowed in case it damages the paint. 'The paint that has already been there nearly fifteen years!' thinks Lewis. He does, however, at least have a lot of shelves where he keeps his vast range of natural history books. Lewis has a strong interest in animals, birds and plants and has already decided that he wants to work in some sort of conservation role.

Standing there, waiting for Jack to look up or at least acknowledge their arrival, Lewis's mind wanders to Tom's unsurprising desire to become a doctor or a science teacher and Jack's ambition to surf in competitions such as the Hawaiian Pro and the Billabong Pipeline Masters, eventually topping the World Surfing League. Lewis can see why his parents often point out that the three of them seem a pretty unlikely match, with their completely differing interests. Even their appearances vary considerably, but something seems to bond them together, and has done since the first year of senior school.

"Yo," Jack greets them, eventually looking up and acknowledging their presence. He closes his laptop and puts it on the floor. Lewis plonks himself down on the end of the bed and Tom, pushing various T-shirts and shorts onto the floor, makes himself comfortable on the wicker seat by the door.

The conversation immediately starts with the haunted cottage on the moor and after Lewis telling them about the spooky things that had happened when his brother Matt had visited, it is very quickly agreed that they will stay overnight also. Matt is only two years older and if he is brave enough to stay, then so are they. It takes a further hour and a half, however, for them to actually agree on a date for when the trip is to take place as various family holidays loom. Eventually the last Wednesday of the school holidays is decided upon.

Mrs Dory is called upstairs, and being assured that there is safety in numbers, she is somehow persuaded by Jack to allow him to go with Tom and Lewis for the overnight adventure on the moor. She doesn't feel she can object; after all, she had always intended to return to the cottage herself as a teenager, hadn't she?

Tom's parents take no persuading. Knowing him to be a sensible, level-headed boy who wouldn't even suggest such a thing if he hadn't already worked out every detail of the trip including the health and safety risks, they agree immediately. However, Tom isn't convinced that his mother is even really listening.

"Nice," is all she murmurs, keying something into her smart phone.

"Yes, yes, make a man of you, son," his father adds condescendingly. Tom secretly wishes that his parents were a little more interested in him. He knows that they care about him, they are just always preoccupied and don't show it very well.

Lewis, however, has a wrangle on his hands. His parents' immediate and joint reaction is a resounding "No!" This is pretty much Lewis's father's stock answer to anything — "Can I…" "No!" "Would it be possible to…" "No!" — before he has even finished his request. Lewis could have been offering his dad a million pounds but no seems to be his automatic response before he hears what is being said. Lewis's dad was brought up on a farm and contrary to popular belief, is not a relaxed outdoors type; he is only too aware of the hazards of the countryside, and of life in general.

What doesn't help either is that his granny also gets into a panic. "You're only a wee lad, you can't be staying out all night in the cold and dark." She makes his parents even more determined to refuse his request. Lewis's saving grace eventually comes in the form of his grandad who fighting his corner, points out that both Jack and Tom have already been granted approval by their parents, stressing Lewis will be teased by them and the rest of the class, if he is considered too young to go.

Listening to her father's opinion and following numerous telephone conversations with both Mrs Dory and Tom's parents over the course of a week, Lewis's mother, Mrs Gordon, finally relents and then persuades her husband into submission. Eventually it is agreed that Lewis can go. His father makes one proviso, however: that he packs warm clothes, his mobile phone, a torch, first aid kit, water, food and bedding and comes straight home the next morning. Thinking it a fairly extensive list to carry all that way for just one night, Lewis knows better than to argue, though, and promises.

Chapter Four

Over the course of the six-week summer holidays Tom spent two sunny, warm weeks lazing, swimming, snorkelling and eating on the Greek island of Santorini. His sisters felt they were too old for family holidays now and his parents, although there in person, continued to spend at least part of each day focussed on work back home.

***

Jack and his mother had gone to the beautiful, Roman city of Bath for a week to stay with a friend of Mrs Dory's, during which time they had visited the famous Roman Baths with their hot springs. Jack had a glass of the natural mineral water that was supposed to be good for your health, but he thought it smelled and tasted like rotten eggs. Disgusted but too polite to spit it out, he had swallowed it, screwing his face up tightly. The best part of the holiday for both Jack and his mum was their trip to the American Museum. Mrs Dory was delighted by the folk and decorative art on display and Jack was fascinated by the exhibitions outlining the culture of the Native American tribes. He spent the day looking at photos of Native Americans and exploring their tepees as well as walking through rooms relating to gangsters and gunslingers of the wild west.

***

Lewis's family couldn't go away for one or two-week's holiday because of all the animals, so his parents and grandparents took it in turns to take him and his siblings out for day trips. They had spent a day at Newquay, eating fish and chips whilst they watched the surfers riding the waves at Fistral Beach. Lewis had thought how odd it was he had never learned to surf despite not only having a huge number of beaches near to where he lived, but also having his friend, Jack, who was such an excellent surfer, so promised himself to do so. They had also driven to Liskeard and taken the train to Looe, where they had wandered the narrow streets, eating pasties and ice creams, whilst looking in shop windows that mostly contained holiday souvenirs. The rest of the time Lewis spent contentedly in the shed at the end of the yard whittling pieces of wood into birds, spoons or porridge spurtles, which he then polished or painted and gave to family and friends as birthday or Christmas gifts.

***

In between family holidays, Tom, Jack and Lewis spent their days together on the beach or at the local skate park. They walked for miles along country lanes and visited megalithic standing stone circles and old wells that had stood there for centuries and had their own folklore stories attached to them. However, the subject of what they considered to be their daring trip to the haunted cottage on the moor was never far from their minds.

Chapter Five

The last week of the holidays finally comes. They say their brief goodbyes to their families and now as the sun is going down, casting a warm orange sheen across the jagged rock covered landscape, Tom, Jack and Lewis, scrabble over and slip on the moss-covered rocks; climb ancient stiles over rough stone walls and trudge through muddy ruts caused by animal trails. Mr and Mrs Gordon had managed to convince the other parents that their boys should also take the safety items deemed important by Lewis's dad. Therefore, the weight of their rucksacks is already dragging down on their shoulders making them tired, hot and sweaty.

It is rough-going underfoot and not for the first time, the boys stop to rest, looking out across the hills and down towards the sparkling diamonds, bouncing and shining on the blue beauty of the Atlantic Sea below. Knowing that it is the right time of year for them to be on their return journey from Scotland, Lewis, sitting down on a boulder amongst the prickly gorse, squints towards the clear, distant sea, ever hopeful that he may see the outline of a huge basking shark. His intense focus is soon interrupted by Tom.

"Let's eat now," he suggests, lowering himself onto a dusty sandy patch of ground beneath a hawthorn tree. Nature loving Lewis's attention is immediately diverted to the tree that is growing at an angle from the rockface, its small red berries indicating the return of autumn. "I'm starving!" Tom says. "And if we eat now, it'll be less to carry."

Jack, always hungry and already fed up with carrying what he felt was a complete overkill in terms of luggage, thinks it's a great idea. "Not just a pretty face," he agrees, winking at Tom.

Ignoring Jack's attempt at humour Tom unzips his rucksack, pulls out sandwiches and crisps and opening the heaviest item in there, he starts guzzling a two-litre bottle of cola. Jack nimbly hops down beside him and there they sit, eating and drinking in silence, looking at the miles and miles of purple, heather covered moorland that surrounds them as the sun sinks yet further over the horizon.

Jumping forward onto his hands and knees Lewis suddenly exclaims, "A devil's coach horse!"

"What? Where?" Jack is on his feet with the agility of an Olympic gymnast, his mouth wide open as he looks around him; his eyes staring like a rabbit caught in the headlights. He has heard the words Devil and horse and thinks they are about to be chased over the moor as the legend foretells.

"Here, numpty. A devil's coach horse. Look!" Lewis and Tom are both peering under the boulder, obviously completely unafraid of any impending pursuit.

"Euwwwww." Tom's face looks like he's eaten something bitter.

Jack leans over the top of them and sees a black beetle with segments of armour and large pincer-like jaws facing them, its head raised, and tail curled over its back like a scorpion ready to defend itself. "Is it dangerous?" Jack asks.

"Only in as much as the smell that it releases when threatened is disgusting," laughs Lewis and deciding to leave the beetle alone he stands up.

The walk takes much longer than they had anticipated, and they argue a few times over whether they are even going in the right direction. It is, therefore, nearly seven o'clock in the evening when the cottage finally comes into view, standing alone, high up on the moor, dwarfed by the imposing dark grey granite rocks and the rugged hills where it has nestled for over two hundred years. Mr Marchant's tales of its sinister reputation were way too tempting for three teenage boys to ignore.

"It doesn't look like much." Jack speaks first, looking at the run-down property ahead of them.

"No, I expected it to look more foreboding," adds Tom.

"Ooh get you, with your big words," laughs Lewis, despite feeling somewhat disappointed that the cottage didn't immediately frighten the wits out of them but at the same time impressed by Tom's use of the English language. "Maybe all the witchy woo wah way stuff is inside," he suggests.

"If there really is any. Like we said before, it might just be Mr M's way of keeping us all off the moor," Jack replies cynically.

First, however, they are going to have to work out how to get into the cottage that is sitting amongst a pile of rocks, rubble and overgrown plants, surrounded by gnarled thorny trees and barbed wire fences. A wooden sign, picturing a skull and cross bones, nailed to a post, leans at an odd angle with the warning 'PRIVATE LAND KEEP OUT' roughly hand painted in red.

"Ugh, do you think that's blood?" Jack asks, looking from Tom to Lewis.

"Don't be daft. It's paint. You're not scared, are you? Either way, we're not backing out now after *that* trek."

Jack, wearing only two-tone shorts and a surf shop T-shirt is feeling the chill of the autumn evening and shivers, but trying to hide his embarrassment, replies, "Of course not. Come on then." He quickly throws his rucksack over the fence, tucks his wavy blond hair back behind his ears and cautiously holding the top row of wire, eases himself between it and the middle row of rusty barbs.

Tom follows suit, but as he leans forward his rucksack catches on the wire, pulling him back rapidly and quickly springing him forward again. The catapult effect causes his black rimmed glasses, selected to match his brown eyes and short dark hair, to shoot forward off his face onto the rough ground before him. "Jack don't move! You'll tread on my glasses," Tom yells worriedly. He tries to pull himself free, but the barbed wire keeps pulling him back "Lewis, quick, untangle me, I'm stuck, and I can't see," he asks.

Lewis is already on the job, carefully pulling out the wire that has hooked itself into the back pocket of Tom's rucksack whilst Jack crawls around on his hands and knees, in the dimming light, feeling in the mud and stones for the glasses. "It's okay, got them" he quickly cries, reaching up to hand them back to a relieved Tom.

Once Tom is successfully through, Lewis follows, also throwing his rucksack over the fence first, having seen the usually organised and composed Tom make the mistake of trying to take the lazy option. He eases himself between the gap, careful not to get the green fine knit top that his grandmother had encouraged him to wear, caught on the sharp wire barbs. She was worried that he would 'catch a chill'.

Treading carefully, all three fumble their way towards the derelict cottage, trousers being grabbed by sharp brambles, their ankles becoming caught in overgrown bindweed or turning on ruts in the ground. They head towards what appears to be the front door, but a steep drop looms, where steps appear to have previously been so, unable to see a way to get down, they retrace their steps back and then around the side of the derelict cottage in search of a back door. The roof and some side walls of the ramshackle cottage have fallen in places, making it even tougher going underfoot, and the boys can't be sure of the stability of what they are walking on. Despite carefully placing their feet, sure enough, there is soon an almighty *crrrrrack* followed by a yell from Lewis as he disappears in front of Tom and Jack's eyes. They scramble as quickly but safely as they can over the rubble and old roof tiles that snap under foot to where they last saw Lewis.

Shining his torch down into a dark, muddy hole about six feet deep, Tom can see his friend, sprawled face down, on a sheet of corrugated roofing that had obviously given way; his right arm above his head with his hand twisted at a funny angle. Lewis is groaning with pain.

"Aargh my arm, my arm, I've broken my arm."

"If he's yelling, at least it means he's alive." Jack is relieved.

"Are you okay?" Tom asks anxiously.

"No, I'm not. I've done something to my arm. Get me out of this flaming hole, *quickly*!" Lewis pleads.

Laying on their bellies, stones digging into their ribs and knees, Tom and Jack reach down into the hole towards Lewis who can only offer up his left hand. Grabbing it, Tom, the taller and broader of the two, pulls with all his might. Lewis screams as his right arm swings by his side. For fear of hurting Lewis further,

Tom instantly lets go. When Lewis is ready to try again, Tom pulls for a second time. On this occasion he manages to drag Lewis about a foot up the mud-lined wall; just enough for Jack to now be able to reach the back of Lewis's jumper. Grasping a handful of blood-spattered material from what would appear to be scratches on Lewis's back, Jack suggests, "Okay try again now," and with one almighty heave they hoist Lewis, his legs scrabbling wildly against the muddy walls, back up out of the hole.

Lewis, grimacing, holds his right elbow in his left hand. "I think I've broken it."

Tom, a member of St John's Ambulance, is trained in first aid and has spent many weekends attending to the sick and injured at sports matches, rock concerts and outdoor festivals. "Can you move your fingers?" he asks.

Lewis wiggles them.

"Hmm, probably not broken then. Let me take a look."

Lewis happily lets Tom examine his arm and watches him admiringly as he works from the shoulder downwards. "Aaargh!" Lewis can't help but scream and he tries to withdraw his arm as Tom reaches his wrist. It is swollen now and getting more painful by the minute.

"I don't think its broken. Could be a hairline fracture of course but you can't tell for sure without an X-ray. Looks more like you've sprained your wrist," Tom suggests.

"Well, that's put an end to that then," Jack sighs.

"Hey, thanks a bunch for your support pal." Lewis winces as he turns towards Jack, the pain shooting up his arm.

"Oh sorry, I didn't mean it like that. I... er... I just meant we'd better get you to a hospital or something." Jack stumbles over his words, trying to make up for what must have looked like a lack of concern at his friend's discomfort.

"Nah, as long as it's not broken, I'll be okay," Lewis assures them, having got this far and not wanting to miss out on the adventure.

Tom looks at him questioningly adding, "You sure? I really think you should get it checked, I'm not a doctor you know."

"Really?" Jack quips. Lewis and Tom both frown at him "Sorry, sorry, just trying to lighten the mood!" Jack holds his hands up as though he is surrendering. Tom tuts and turns his back on Lewis, surprised at Jack's further lack of tact and diplomacy.

"Yeah, I'm pretty sure," Lewis once again confirms, more hopeful than really convinced but not wanting to miss out on the opportunity of spending this trip with the clever and highly skilled Tom.

Tom opens his rucksack and pulls out a professional looking green plastic box with a white cross stamped on it and the words 'First Aid.' Jack smiles inwardly; the first aid kit his mother packed him consists solely of some plasters, cotton wool balls and a bottle of antiseptic liquid. 'Not much use unless I regress to the age of five, fall over in the playground and graze my knee,' he thinks, batting his eyes. Pulling a crepe bandage out from a substantial number of supplies Tom then says confidently, "I'll strap it up for you. The support will reduce the swelling and lessen the pain."

With just a few swift movements Lewis's arm is in a sling, his wrist held securely against his chest. Trying to put on a brave face but becoming ever more aware of the increasing pain, Lewis prises the lid off a white plastic lunch box with his left hand and looks for some pain killers amongst the equally well-stocked first aid kit his father has sent him off with.

Chapter Six

With more than just Lewis's pride hurt, they take extra care walking to the rear of the cottage. The old unpainted wooden door displays another hand painted sign that simply reads KEEP OUT. The door is already partly open, and Jack, using his lantern to see, cautiously pokes his head around the gap to look inside, creaking and scuffing the bottom of the door as he pushes hard to open it further. Jack has always gone first when the three of them go anywhere. Everyone thinks he is super cool — typical golden tan, long wavy blond hair, mega skills at surf and skateboarding. The trouble is, Jack has now started believing it too and seems to think it's his right to lead.

All three are oozing with anticipation as one after the other, they enter the first room in the cottage. The bare wooden floor is missing some of its floorboards, showing a mixture of mud and stone in the gaps beneath. Most of the roof is missing and windows that had previously been glazed are now merely open holes in the walls with ivy climbing through, gripping the stone like green octopus tentacles reaching their way into the room.

It is old, cold and damp, but not in the least bit scary.

Shining their respective torches and lanterns around the walls, Tom, Jack and Lewis can see graffiti that has been chalked on, or carved into the stone: 'R luvs T 1986'; 'Get Out Quick — this place is haunted'; and 'Josh and Zac woz ere 2006' along with more pictures of skulls and crossbones or danger zig zags drawn by previous visitors who, like them, had 'dared' to enter the cottage.

Tom, Jack and Lewis stand there in silence. They had each expected to feel something special — if not totally petrified then at least an eerie uneasiness — but all three feel nothing other than a tinge of disappointment. It is just a run-down old cottage, pretty much the same as any other derelict property. The only difference is that this one sits alone, high up on a moor, out of view of any other houses, and of course, horrible things have allegedly happened here in the past.

Sensing the somewhat flat atmosphere and despite the pain he has endured getting here, Lewis, ever the optimist, tries to sound cheery and says hopefully "I know it doesn't look much but we've only just come in. Maybe it'll be better further inside."

"Yeah, and when it's fully dark," chips in Jack.

So, together, they walk silently into the next room, scanning the bare walls. As they enter a room in the middle of the cottage Jack stops and slowly allows the light from his lantern to travel from the floor to the ceiling of the facing wall. The hairs on his arms stand on end as the lantern reveals a five-sided star about four feet tall daubed in black in the centre of the wall.

"This is more like it. A pentagram," Tom announces knowledgeably.

"Pentagrams are a sign of evil, aren't they?" Jack asks, having heard something about pentagrams being a Satanic symbol.

"Not really! The symbol was used in the past by the ancient Greeks, Babylonians and the Christians, as a sign of faith. It's more often associated with pagans and wiccans nowadays though." Tom explains.

"Wiccans are witches," Jack states, as though he has proved his point.

"Not like you understand witches to be, they're not. You really should study a bit more you know," Tom corrects Jack.

"So why do people say its evil then?" Jack quizzes Tom further.

"Well!" Tom replies, having learned a lot about pagan and wiccan beliefs as well as the more sinister side of black magic, when he was searching for information regarding the legends surrounding this cottage. "People misunderstand. For pagans, the five points of the star actually represent life force or energy: earth, air, fire and water with spirit being the point at the top. But in horror films and books they sometimes turn it upside down so that the point is at the bottom to indicate evil or hell." Tom did a great deal of reading about a great many subjects. Looking at the pentagram again he further adds, "Maybe on this occasion they did intend it as a Satanic symbol though. See! The centre point is facing downwards."

Excitement increasing amongst them all now, Jack turns his lantern to his right and painted on the wall facing them, are three intertwined black snakes with red eyes. A scan of the remaining two walls reveal upside down crosses, which they all know are also sometimes used to represent evil. There are also painted representations of black cats with yellow eyes flashing anger; their claws extended, reaching out in various threatening poses.

"Cripes, this is actually some seriously creepy stuff," says Tom, somewhat taken aback. He isn't, however, feeling the same level of fear that is now beginning to seep through Jack's bones.

"What's that?" Lewis suddenly asks, having heard deep throaty roars echoing across the moor.

"Very funny," Jack replies, thinking that Lewis is winding him up.

"No, really. Listen! What is it?"

Standing as still as statues, all three tilt their heads to one side as they try to identify the sound Lewis has heard. Sure enough, somewhere in the distance, pulsating deep rumbling growls subside one by one to silence.

"What the heck was that?" Jack is already conjuring up pictures in his mind of prides of prowling lions or worse still, monstrous sabre-toothed tigers.

Tom shrugs his shoulders and raising his eyebrows, pulls a face indicating that he doesn't have a clue. All three remain quiet and continue listening.

Despite Lewis trying to allay their fears by suggesting a number of perfectly normal reasons for the noise, Jack is visibly shaken and even the usually calm, realistic Tom isn't so sure that they are not in danger. He therefore suggests that instead of moving on to check out the rest of the cottage, they should stay where they are and go no further until they are sure that whatever it is, has gone away. Sitting down in the middle of the room, on the cold hard stone floor, heads cocked to one side, not speaking, they listen intently for over an hour. Just as they settle, realising that nothing scary has happened and accepting Lewis's reasonable explanations for the roar, Tom puts his finger to his lips, whispering quietly, "Shhh."

"What is it? Is it back?" Jack looks shocked.

"It sounds like voices outside," Tom replies.

Not wanting to be caught unprepared for whatever may face them, Tom immediately stands up, and seeing Lewis struggling to do the same, pulls him up by his one good arm. Jack doesn't want to face whatever it is that Tom has heard outside and remains sitting on the floor, hugging his rucksack defensively. However, as soon as Tom and Lewis walk out of the room, leaving him alone, he quickly jumps to follow them. He catches them up as they re-enter the first room, bumping straight into Tom's back, who has stopped abruptly.

All three tense and looking over Tom's shoulder, Jack gasps. The doorframe is filled by a huge dark bulky figure.

"All right!" It's more of a statement than a question. The greeting is so casual that Tom immediately relaxes and lifts his lantern.

Clomping towards them in heavy biker boots is a very tall and enormously beefy looking man wearing black leather trousers and a black leather jacket with a denim waistcoat jacket with cut-off sleeves over the top. His head is shaved, and his face is completely covered by a tattoo of a black spider's web. He looks fearsome, making Tom tense again. He looks way more frightening than the paintings they had just seen on the walls.

Lumbering in after him comes a second man, dressed the same. This one has long wavy black hair and three teardrops tattooed under each eye. Then another man, and another, and another. The last is carrying something large hidden under his jacket. Soon there are eight big, burly bikers crowding the tiny room, all dressed in leather and denims and all sporting different tattoos on their faces and necks.

Taken aback and trying to assess whether they are in danger from what is obviously a biker gang, Lewis, already feeling vulnerable due to his strongest arm being in a sling, can only stand and stare, whilst Tom makes a crooked, and rather poor, attempt at a smile. Jack, however, grabbing the back of Tom's shoulders, is twitching and has a heavy feeling in the pit of his stomach. Trying to then back away he feels a sharp stab in his right shoulder blade but soon forgets the pain as his mind turns to television programmes he has seen where Hells Angels kill competing gang members over turf or drugs wars. Maybe these bikers live here, and they are trespassing in their home. His mind races with thoughts of what horrors might now happen.

The first man speaks. "Any good?" He is looking past Tom and directly at Jack who visibly jumps, causing the man to laugh. "Ah, so some pretty spooky stuff in here then, is there?"

"N-n-no, n-n-n-not really." Tom answers for Jack who is standing there with his jaw dropped, his mouth wide open like a fish gasping for air.

"What about all the so called Satanic, evil stuff?" the man persists.

Tom points towards the next room. "S-s-some st-st-stuff on the walls in there."

Spiderweb man walks up to them and Lewis, looking like a rabbit caught in the headlights, only manages to jump out of the way when the man, waiting for him to move, stops in front of him, looks him straight in the eye and coughs. The rest of the bikers follow, their chunky boots crunching across the wooden floor into the middle room.

"Let's run," Jack whispers.

"Run? Why?" asks Tom.

"Because of the Angels." Jack nods towards the centre of the cottage, adding, "Didn't you see the bulge under the last guy's jacket? Probably guns and machetes and stuff. They might stab us or shoot us or something, come on, quick!"

Heavy footsteps accompanied by deep voices and laughing resound inside the cottage. Then they smell burning.

"See! They're laughing at what they are going to do to us. They're going to burn us at the stake. Come on before it's too late," Jack pleads.

But it is already too late, as dipping his head to get back through the small doorway into the room, the man is peering at them through the black spider's web tattoo. Saying nothing, he merely nods. A broad grin grows across the biker's face as he takes one step towards Jack, slapping him on the shoulder. Feeling a sense of dread, Jack starts laughing nervously. Tom and Lewis stare at him wondering what he is laughing at. Jack doesn't want to laugh. He certainly doesn't feel like laughing. He doesn't even know why he is laughing or what he is laughing at, but he can't stop. The biker nods again and turning Jack around, guides him back to the middle room of the cottage.

"You two, this way," he directs Tom and Lewis. Knowing that they have no chance against a gang of bikers, Tom immediately follows, grabbing the front of

Lewis's jumper and pulling him behind him. The rest of the gang are sitting around a small fire in the centre of the room. His hand still on Jack's shoulder the spiderweb man says, "Guys, this is…" He waits for Jack to introduce himself, but Jack just stands there, visibly shaking.

"Jack," says Tom quickly. "He's Jack and I'm Tom. This is Lewis," he adds, again pulling Lewis alongside.

"Pull up a chair," another biker suggests. Tom looks at the tattoo of barbed wire that trails down one side of his face onto his neck, disappearing beneath his leather jacket. The gang all laugh at his joke. The only option for sitting is, like them, on the floor.

"Uh, yeah, thanks, will do," Tom replies, taking the lead and sitting down as far away from them as the small room allows.

Spiderweb man looks at Lewis then at Jack and raises his eyebrows questioningly. They both sit down immediately.

"W-w-what are you going to do to us?" Jack stutters.

"Do?" Spiderweb man looks at him. Then he laughs. A loud deep-throated laugh. "I'll tell you exactly what we're going to do."

Jack screws his face up and shuts his eyes so he doesn't have to see what is going to happen next. Lewis places his hand on his chest, trying to still his beating heart and Tom swallows hard. *Bonk!* Something hard hits Tom on the arm, and bouncing off, lands on the floor. Jack jumps and hearing the thud squeezes his eyes even more tightly shut. He really doesn't want to see the torture that one of his friends is obviously already being subjected to.

"Cheers, mate," spiderweb man calls out.

Jack half opens one eye and peers through the foggy curtain of his eyelashes. The biker with the weapons is putting his hand inside his jacket and pulling something out. 'That's it,' thinks Jack, quickly closing both eyes again, 'we're dead.'

The bikers are all smiling as Tom, with a huge sense of relief, looks at the offending item on the floor and realises they have thrown him a can of beer.

"Oh, uh, thank you," Tom replies as two more cans are thrown across.

Lewis picks his up in his one good hand. Spotting Lewis's dilemma as he looks at the can, trying to work out how to pull the tab at the same time as hold it, the biker nearest him leans across, takes it from him, opens it and hands it back silently.

"Thanks," Lewis says, "that's very kind of you."

Jack however still has his eyes closed, his shoulders hunched tightly up against his neck and his long wavy blond hair flopping forward.

Tom pushes him. "Say thank you."

Jack again only opens one eye but seeing the can on the floor in front him and that no one has been shot, stabbed or beheaded, flicks his hair back and tries to act suddenly cool. "Hey, yeah, thanks."

Relieved, Tom, Jack and Lewis sip at their beers, trying to look cool, but not really liking the bitter taste. Laughing, the bikers make space for them around the fire and soon throw them each another can. "You were right, guys. A totally wasted hike up here. Nothing scary at all." Spiderweb man looks a bit frustrated.

"You three staying the night?" another asks.

"Yeah, we thought it would be pretty dope," Jack answers, trying to regain some street cred.

The bikers chat amongst themselves about their bikes, the walk up and the cottage for about another hour or so and Tom, Jack and Lewis soon learn a lot about Triumph and Norton motorcycles. They listen intently, feeling a bit woozy after two cans. Then, standing up, Spiderweb man stomps on the flames with one large heavy black boot. "Better not leave you kids alone with an open fire."

Taking offence Tom nearly argues that they are not kids, but looking at the rest of the bikers all now standing above them, thinks better of it.

With that, the eight leather clad guys, each raising a hand but not saying a word, duck through the doorway and walk out through the cottage and into the darkness. The three teenagers follow them to the back door, watching them clambering over the rocks and away into the darkness.

"It's a trick," mumbles Jack. "They tried to get us drunk 'cause they're playing with us. They'll be back any minute or perhaps they're waiting to kill us in our sleep."

"Just shut it and get real Jack," Tom replies angrily, "You can hear those boots clanking down over the rocks a mile away."

"Ah, but maybe one or two have stayed behind." Jack is obviously still not convinced but it is too dark to see so all they can do is stand with their backs against the outside wall and listen until a long time later when far, far in the distance they again hear the familiar, throaty rumble and thundering growl.

"Motorbikes, of course. That's what the noise was in the first place." Lewis starts laughing. He laughs so hard and for so long, that Tom, and even Jack soon join him. Bent double and gasping for breath, until Tom exclaims "They're not actually riding those bikes after drinking, are they?" He looks worried, knowing that not only is it illegal but that they could do themselves or, possibly worse still, others, terrible harm.

Chapter Seven

After a while, Lewis spots that Tom is staring into the middle distance, deep in thought about the previous occupants of the cottage.

"What a nightmare," Tom says out of the blue.

Looking around him quickly, thinking he has overlooked something important and potentially scary Lewis asks, "What? What's a nightmare?" quickly determining that if Tom isn't panicking, he's going to do his best not to.

Absent-mindedly Tom replies, "Having to carry the shopping all the way up here."

Lewis grins at Tom. Trust him to think of the practical implications of living so far up on the moor.

Their previous fear explained and therefore now completely gone, and their good humour restored, the boys return inside. No one mentions it but they all feel complete numpties for having thought the rumbling sound and the bikers so scary. The bikers had actually been really nice guys, who had shared their beers with them, albeit they did seem to have had a bit of a joke at Jack's expense. Having as yet still got no further than the middle room, they each pick up their rucksacks and venture deeper into the cottage.

Jack, knowing that he needs to do something to regain his cool image, again leads the way into what appears to be an old kitchen. Catching a dark burgundy red patch in his light, he again tucks his hair behind one ear to better study it and taps the floor with his converse trainer. "Ugh! Looks like old blood. Perhaps we shouldn't stay after all!" he says, by way of a statement more than a question. He has already started feeling a bit jittery again.

"Something must've died in here," Tom teases as shivers travel down Jack's spine, adding, "I'd be more worried about the blood on your T-shirt."

Jack turns, his blue eyes open so wide they look like saucers and then he remembers having jabbed his back on something in the doorway earlier. He whips off his T-shirt. "Must've snagged it on a nail or splinter or something," he concludes, pulling the T-shirt back over his head again.

Lewis, ignoring all talk of blood, overtakes Jack and going ahead alone, finds a room at the back of the cottage where, painted in white on the floor, is the faint outline of a large circle with an eye drawn in the middle. It is surrounded by numbers then another outer circle containing letters. "Whoa creepy as…" he says out loud to no one but himself and then calls out, "Hey, guys, come and look in here. There's a Ouija! This is awesome."

Wanting to see the subject of Lewis's enthusiasm, Tom and Jack join him.

"D'you mean one of those things you use to contact the dead? I thought they were boards or something?" Jack replies, hoping that it isn't.

"Looks the same to me, just bigger, innit!" Lewis confirms.

As it is the only room with a roof remaining, against Jack's wishes, Tom and Lewis agree it is the best place to settle for the night, Ouija or not. They place their sleeping bags around the outside edge of the circle, each one instinctively feeling a need to keep some distance from it.

Remembering Mr Marchant's tales that had brought them here, the three soon start taking it in turns to tell stories of the spriggans who sometimes trick people and lead them astray to be lost for ever on the moors; of the Cornish knockers who inhabit the old mine shafts and steal people's belongings; and the fae folk that people have spotted when out walking but who no one else could see. Their tales eventually turn to the occultist who had previously owned the cottage.

"He was known as the Dark Conjurer." Tom explains.

"Who summoned the workers of the very Devil himself," Lewis elaborates, with a poor impression of his Scottish granny who had told him of the local newspaper report from many years ago. Sitting crossed legged on folded sleeping bags, they all laugh; even Jack seems to have forgotten his earlier fears.

They talk on into the night, continuing with reports of the suspicious sudden deaths and suicides that befell anyone who had visited its infamous owner.

"A woman who lived over the hills died after attending a séance with him," Lewis explains, further adding, "She fell to the floor shaking, her fists clenched, her eyes rolling, and froth was coming out of her mouth." He squirms around on the floor, dribbling as he re-enacts the picture he is painting.

Jack laughs at the sight of Lewis with his arm in a sling, trying to roll only on one side on the ground.

Tom, however, is unimpressed and remarks, "It sounds like a fairly standard seizure to me."

Undeterred, Lewis sits up and continues. "Ah, but then another lady died at a black mass here. She was made to kneel on the floor in front of men in black hoods and cloaks holding long wooden staffs covered in jewels. They chanted magic words at her that only they could understand and then when black smoke came out of the high priest's mouth, his face changed before her and her eyes and ears poured with blood, she fell backwards and bang. She was dead."

Further and further into the night they compete with more gruesome tales of witchcraft and blood sacrifices, until, eventually, due to a mixture of nerves and excitement, their spines tingling, Tom concludes, "The Dark Conjurer only died himself after drinking the poisoned blood of one of his sacrifices."

This seems to bring the talk to a natural close and sitting in silence, they soak up the atmosphere of the cottage and contemplate the actions of its previous infamous occupant.

Tom jumps as Lewis suddenly blurts out, "Hey, as we're here, this Ouija is an opportunity too good to miss. Let's have a go."

"Yeah, we could try contacting family who have passed over," Tom suggests.

"Or better still, how about the people who died here?" Jack adds, full of bravado.

"Don't we need a glass or something?" Tom questions.

Lewis reaches into his rucksack and brings out a purple plastic beaker. "Ta da. Close as," he smiles, placing it on the Ouija.

Sitting around the outside edge of the chalk circle, each with a lit torch or lantern next to them, Jack and Tom follow Lewis's lead and place an index finger on the upturned cup.

"Is there anybody there?" Lewis asks in an exaggeratedly scary voice.

Nothing happens.

Lewis asks again, "Is there anybody there?"

They wait. Silence! All three feel equally embarrassed at how ridiculous they must look with their fingers on a purple beaker asking the dead to speak to them. They start giggling until the cup wobbles slightly and very slowly slides across to the letter Y. They jump and instantly snatch their fingers away from the upturned cup.

"It must mean yes." Lewis states the obvious.

They wait and when nothing more happens Tom suggests, "Ask it something else."

They replace their fingers and undeterred, Lewis calls out, "Is there somebody here with us?"

Again, the cup trembles and moves across the circle on the stone floor to the letter G. The three don't move this time but look at each other wide-eyed. The cup moves on, very gradually sliding over to B, then on to M.

Jack's heart is racing, and his mouth has gone dry. "Don't ask it any more," he pleads, hoping desperately that it's one of the other two pushing the cup as a joke and not really a dead person speaking to them. Either way he's feeling spooked, and regretting having agreed to this.

Tom and Lewis are also now on edge and breaking the silence, Lewis asks, "GBM! What's that supposed to mean?"

Jack shakes his head and looks at the floor.

Tom ponders over the letters and suggests, "Gory Black Masses?"

Lewis laughs but Jack doesn't think it's funny. He doesn't want to engage any more.

"Or Great Big Murderer," Lewis adds. "Or Gert Big Monster; or Grave Before Midnight; Giant Black and Macabre."

"All right, all right we've got the gist." Tom elbows him, smiling, then looks subdued again as he too considers the very unlikely possibility that it might not be one of his friends pushing the cup. Tom, looking like he's just had a eureka moment suddenly exclaims, "It's my grandfather's initials. G. B. M. George Bartholomew Milton."

Lewis starts laughing uncontrollably this time. "Bartholomew! That's it! That's what the B is in the initials on your PE shirt. TBM. Thomas *Bartholomew* Milton. No wonder you wouldn't tell us. Bartholomew, ha, ha, ha!" Lewis quite likes the name really but doesn't want to show it. He thinks it has a rather distinguished air to it and to Lewis's mind it suits Tom well.

Jack forces a little smile but cuts the humour short as he blurts out, "B-b-but all your grandparents are dead, aren't they?" He immediately regrets having asked the question as he already knows he doesn't want to hear the answer.

Tom's expression turns to one of confusion and concerned by the implication he nods, replying simply, "Uh yeah, they are."

Lewis is also brought back down to earth both by concern that Tom may be upset by the mention of his dead grandparents and by the thought of his own grandparents; his father's parents, who have both passed away. Having heard about séances from his Scottish granny, Lewis is quick to accept that the spirit in the room with them may well be Tom's grandfather and carefully encourages Tom to ask for more information in case GBM has important information for him. However, no matter how many times Tom asks, and in how many different ways, the cup doesn't move again. Not knowing what else to ask, they all sit and wait quietly.

Tom, still not really believing what he has just seen, tries to think of other explanations for the cup moving.

Not ready to give up yet, Lewis suggests, "You try, Jack."

Jack shakes his head.

"Oh, come on. It's your turn. We've both done it. Ask it something," Lewis further encourages.

Reluctantly, with their fingers back on the cup, Jack very quietly asks, "Do you have a message for us?"

The plastic cup trembles and moves again, to the letter D. It slides across the ground to the letter I. Their fingers held steady on the cup it slowly traces across the circle to the E.

"Wh-h-ho did that, stop pushing it," pleads Jack, his jaw clenching. They wait for the next letter, but it stops. D.I.E. "DIE! Whoa that's not funny." Jack's face has turned white, and he looks like he is going to pass out.

Both Lewis and Tom now decide that the other really must be making the cup move to put the frighteners up Jack. They start pushing each other and laughing, arguing back and forth. "Eejit, stop it."

"It's not me. It's you."

Neither admits responsibility so eventually Lewis, still unshaken and determined to deflect any giveaway signs of his secret admiration, insists, "Ask it again, it must be a mistake. Maybe there's a T to come. Tom's carrying a bit of extra timber so it's probably a message from his grandfather. Go on a diet." Lewis doubles over, amused at his own joke.

Jack, shaking his head, takes his finger off the cup and leans back, adamant that he longer wants to be involved.

Half nervous and half intrigued, Lewis repeats, "Do you have a message for us?"

He returns the upturned cup to the centre and with just his and Tom's fingers now resting on it, it moves again, slowly at first, to the letter J and on to D. Just as slowly it returns to the centre but then swiftly moves back to the letter D again. Without stopping it quickly shoots across to I and comes to rest at E.

Jack can't breathe. He feels like ice cold water is running through his veins. J.D DIE. His initials. Jack Dory. The message is for him: 'Jack Dory Die'. All three now feel apprehensive, concerned by the repeated message. Tom and Lewis instinctively feel that something powerful, frightening and significant may have just happened and are no longer inclined to think the other is to blame. Without speaking they take their fingers off, and as one, they silently shuffle back and lean against the wall, as far away from the Ouija as they can get.

As the night wears on Jack manages to convince himself that either Tom or Lewis had undoubtedly been messing around, making the cup move. Tom and Lewis, believing any alternative extremely unlikely, also return to their original belief that the other is to blame and revert to again playfully accusing each other.

"It *was* you, wasn't it?"

The reply is always, "No! It was *you*!"

In short, eventually none of them believe that the messages were real, and they start to relax.

Deliberately avoiding the subject of the Ouija, scary stories or indeed the cottage itself, they decide to play safe by avoiding all conversation and snuggle into their sleeping bags.

"Awesome!" Jack suddenly exclaims, waving a red foil shaped heart in the air. He doesn't mention the small hand-written note he has just found wrapped around it in his sleeping bag.

'I love you, sexy dude! A xxxxxxxxx'

"Amelie is such a soppy girl" he says grinning broadly, extremely pumped and proud of the fact that his girlfriend must have slipped a surprise gift into his sleeping bag when they had said their goodbyes. Jack loves chocolate and guzzles the bite size piece in one.

Tom, meanwhile, is laying on his back clutching a copy of the *Complete Revision and Practice GCSE Maths* book to his chest. Mia had given it to him in preparation for next year's exams, encouraging him to bring it with him, thinking he might have spare time on his hands. Not that that has proved possible so far. It reminds him of her though, so it makes him feel comfortable just having it there.

Lewis is having an internal battle deliberating over when to give Tom the gift he has made for him or whether he should even give it to him at all. He decides to wait until Jack isn't around. He doesn't want him taking the mickey.

Eventually, silently and one by one, they fall asleep.

Chapter Eight

Jack wakes up with a start. He can hear breathy whistling interspersed with a horrible panting sound close by. He pricks his ears and listens carefully. The noise is in the room. His palms are sweaty as he quietly moves his hand around inside his sleeping bag, feeling for the torch that he had the sense to put in earlier so he could find it quickly should he need it. It is by his hip. He moves his fingers over it, feels the rubber ON/OFF button and presses it. A dim light seeps through the material of the sleeping bag. The breath is getting faster and rasping. Pulling the torch out very slowly, Jack shines it in the direction he can hear the sound coming from.

It is Lewis. His head has rolled back onto his shoulders, his nostrils are flaring, and his breathing is getting faster and faster as he gasps for air.

"Tom, Tom, wake up, wake up," Jack shouts, panic stricken at seeing his friend like this.

Tom has been in a deep sleep and feels a bit groggy but doing his best to come round, he forces his eyelids open. Jack, still in his sleeping bag, is too afraid to approach Lewis and continues staring at him with a mixture of fear and concern.

"Tom, it's Lewis. I think it's the Ouija message. It's coming true. I thought it meant me but it's Lewis. Quick! He's going to die."

Tom is now up, out of his sleeping bag and across the room before Jack finishes his sentence.

Lewis is struggling to speak, his chest moving in and out rapidly "I… can't… breathe. I… can't…"

"Oh no! He's been possessed by the Devil and he's having a seizure like that lady, isn't he?" Jack just stares at Lewis, his eyes wide open, thinking that the stories about the cottage must be true and some horrific scene is about to play out in front of him.

"That's really not helpful." Tom shoots Jack an angry look. "He's having an asthma attack. Come on, Jack. You've seen it happen enough times before."

Lewis's only useful hand is flapping around near his rucksack, desperately grappling to find the zip. Tom very swiftly but very calmly takes the bag from him, unzips it and has the inhaler out and into Lewis's hand in no time. Lewis takes one deep puff on it and his breathing starts to slow. He slumps back against the wall, taking long, laboured, painful breaths. Jack is so relieved he looks like he is about to cry. Yet again he is also embarrassed that his fear has got the better of him, and in this case, has overridden any attempt to help his friend.

When Lewis's breathing settles into a normal rhythm, Tom directs the light from his lantern onto the black spots creeping up the grey stone wall, advising,

"Now get away from the wall. Look at all that mould. That's probably what set you off." This time, worried about both Lewis's arm and now also his asthma attack, even Tom is beginning to think that maybe enough is enough. They have done what they set out to do and slept, if not overnight, then at least part of the night, in the cottage and even he now wishes they could call it a day and go home. But looking at the windowless hole in the wall he can see that it is still pitch-black outside — too dark and too dangerous to climb back down over the rocks. He shuffles closer to the centre of the room, the end of his sleeping bag laying just within the outer circle of the Ouija.

Lewis follows, grateful as always that he has such a special friend in Tom. A friend who always manages to be there for him. Jack, however, remains with his head close to the wall. Mould or no mould, he is determined to keep as much distance from the Ouija as he can.

With his inhaler still clutched in his hand and knowing that Tom is always looking out for him, Lewis eventually drifts off to sleep, soon followed by Tom. Disturbed by the tales they had told each other, and once again convinced that no good can come of their visit to the cottage, Jack lays there for longer before the tiredness of the long walk, the beer and repeat anxiety finally takes its toll, and he too nods off.

Jack's sleep, however, is fitful, and he tosses and turns in his sleeping bag, drifting back and forth between the hazy world of dreaming, dozing and nearly, but not fully, awake. He grabs his neck as his heart feels like it has leapt into his throat and is going to choke him. Blood curdling screams are coming from outside.

"W-w-w-what's that?" he can just about manage to whisper.

Tom, also now awake, sits up abruptly, holds his breath and listens. His muscles tense and his heart thuds in his chest as the pitiful screaming continues.

Lewis, too, has been disturbed and is awake but hasn't bothered to lift his head. "Cool it, guys, it's only the wind blowing through the dolmen." Lewis is familiar with the strange sound. He has heard how the wind whistles through the granite stones many times in the past, when he went hiking on the moor with his father and his brother Matt. However, he does agree that it sounds more eerie in the dark.

"Dolmen?" Tom asks, his heart slowing, immediately relieved that Lewis sounds so relaxed about it.

"Yeah. Dolmens are Neolithic burial chambers," Lewis adds knowledgably.

"W-w-w-what? Erm, you mean for like, uh, d-d-d-dead people?" Jack stammers, still finding it hard to speak as his dry tongue is sticking to the roof of his mouth.

"Duh, I hope so. I think burying people alive is kind of like illegal," Tom teases Jack.

Both Lewis and Tom start laughing but Jack looks serious; he is more concerned about the screaming coming from the burial chamber than pretending to join in with their humour at his expense. After all, he thinks, it might not just be the wind.

Only moments later, as the screaming wind continues, they hear a scratching sound, *shtck shtck shtck*. This time not only Jack but also Tom and Lewis freeze. The hairs go up on the back of Lewis's neck. Jack, who it is now clearly apparent to both Tom and Lewis is not anything like as cool as they, or indeed anyone else at school, had previously thought, grabs his torch, and clenches it in front of his chest like a weapon. *Shtck shtck shtck.* The scratching continues.

"It's in the c-c-c-c-cottage," Jack mutters, his spare hand immediately covering his open mouth.

Even Lewis is more scared than his very calmly asked question implies. "What do you suppose it is?"

Tom shrugs and feels equally uneasy.

"I'd better go and check it out," suggests Lewis bravely.

"Oh no you don't. You've only got one good hand and that won't be much use in a fight." Tom tries to sound light-hearted about the situation. As much as he doesn't want to go himself, Tom can see that no one is going to be able to get back to sleep if they feel trapped in a small room at the back of an old, derelict cottage on a moor in the dead of night, not knowing what is causing the scratching sound. He therefore insists that he will go and holding his lantern out in front of him, he walks out of the room. Jack is too petrified to even consider feeling embarrassed about leaving Tom to check alone and Lewis is undecided about how much support he would be in any case, with his arm in a sling and having just got over an asthma attack.

His heart pounding in his chest and his head thumping in time, Tom treads very carefully through the dark rooms lit only by the faint glow of his lantern. He is not feeling anything like as brave as he appears, but he has to figure out what is causing the noise. *Shtck shtck shtck.* The sound makes him visibly shiver. It reminds him of something heavy being slowly dragged across a floor, like a dead body maybe. Goose pimples rise on his forearms and the back of his neck. *Shtck shtck shtck.* He turns into the last room and is back by the open door at the rear of the cottage. Raising his lantern, he stops suddenly, swallows hard and gasps as two large dark eyes stare widely at him. Again, his heart leaps in his chest. It is not as big as him, but it's large enough and it's alive. The thing stands its ground, black eyes fixed firmly on Tom. Then, suddenly, with a burst of energy it jumps, turns and runs, straight out of the door, away from him.

Tom had thought for a moment that whatever it was, was coming for him and the shock of the sudden movement has made him feel a little nauseous. Panting, he bends over, his hands on his knees as he tries to catch his breath. Eventually his pulse starts to gradually slow, and he grins to himself. 'A sheep, nothing but a freaking sheep.' It had been scratching its thick woolly coat on the rough, splintered doorframe.

Tom stands there for several minutes, catching his breath and regaining his composure. He really thought he was done for, for a moment there. He is about to call out to Jack and Lewis but as his so-called mates didn't have the guts to even come with him as a bit of back-up, he decides to remain silent and has an idea. He walks out through the open door and with his torch off and his hand dragging along the cottage wall to give him an idea of direction, Tom quietly picks his way over the uneven ground and creeps around to the other side of the building.

Some time passes and although the scratching sound has stopped, Jack and Lewis still don't know what caused it and Tom is still not back. Lewis suggests, therefore, that despite his fear, they have no choice but to go and check that Tom is okay. After all, Tom always helps him. Jack tries to resist, offering numerous reasons as to why they should stay where they are and wait for Tom to return, but Lewis, fearing for Tom's safety, insists that they should both go. He isn't feeling that brave himself and would much rather there were two of them. They walk slowly through the cottage, treading carefully on the broken floorboards quietly calling out for Tom. There is no sign of him. They too end up outside the cottage and with torches and lanterns in hand they stand looking out onto the dark moorland where black menacing shadows of rocky outcrops and huge granite standing stones look like giant monsters bearing down on them. There are no other properties around and not even a single sign of a house light in the distance.

"Tom," Lewis whispers quietly, afraid of what may hear him out there in the darkness. There is no reply. "Tom, where are you?" he calls again worriedly, a little louder this time. Still nothing. Afraid to venture too far from the cottage, they remain where they are. Waiting. A blood-curdling screech sounds again in the distance. Lewis cocks his head. It is different to the wailing of the wind through the dolmen. This sounds like a woman screaming. Both Lewis and Jack instinctively back into the doorway, pressed shoulder to shoulder in the narrow gap. The woman screams again, a dreadful, agonising, harrowing yell, that echoes far into the dark night.

"Oh no, please, please no." Lewis feels choked with guilt at leaving their best friend to go and check alone. They have no idea where Tom is, and his mind, conjuring up pictures of a woman being attacked by a ferocious animal, or something even more sinister, starts whirling out of control as he suspects that it has already done far worse to the missing, caring, brave Tom.

Jack, too, is picturing the horrific scene that must be taking place out on the moor to cause the woman to scream so distressingly. But he is more concerned about his own safety and is challenging his brain to work a way out of this terrifying situation. He wishes he had never come. He wants to go home where he is safe. He doesn't care that it is dark and therefore dangerous to embark on a journey back down the hazardous hillside of loose rocks. He doesn't care that his rucksack with his belongings is still inside. He has to get away and he is determined that he is going now. He starts to gradually inch his way forwards out of the doorway into the cottage grounds.

"Where are you going?" asks Lewis, presuming that Jack is acting bravely and going to either search for Tom or to somehow help the screaming woman.

"Home," Jack replies simply.

"You can't go now, you idiot. We haven't found Tom and anyway, you'll break your neck out there," Lewis declares.

"I can and I am," Jack snaps as something jumps out of the hedgerow and up onto the wall immediately to their right.

'Ow-wow-wow,' it yips causing Jack to quickly scuttle backwards into the doorway alongside Lewis who yells as Jack, in his rush, elbows him into the doorframe, jolting his injured wrist. Still wincing with pain, Lewis quickly shines his light on the animal who turns its startled, shining yellow eyes towards them and then promptly jumps off the wall and disappears amongst the black shadows of the gorse and heather.

"Phew, it's only a fox." Jack relaxes, having caught a quick glimpse of the fleeing animal.

"Does that mean you can let go of my sleeve now? Lewis asks sarcastically.

Jack hadn't even noticed that, in his panic, he had grabbed Lewis's jumper like a frightened child catching hold of his mother's skirt. Embarrassed, he apologises, not knowing what else to say other than, "But what about the screaming?" His muscles immediately tense at the thought once more. "I've just realised, I should've recognised it earlier. It's a vixen. A female fox calling for a mate. That's why the male barked back." Greatly relieved and grinning shyly at their foolishness, the two turn and head back inside. Lewis however is desperately worried. Tom has not replied to their calls, but he knows deep down that it would be treacherous to go searching far from the cottage.

Back in the Ouija room Lewis decides the only thing they can do is phone for help, but he can't decide who to call. If he calls his older brother, Matt, he'll just laugh and think it's a joke or that he's being a big coward for not going out to search for Tom himself. If he calls his father, it will only prove him right that Lewis shouldn't have been allowed to go as he had instructed in the first place. If he calls the police, they may all get in trouble because they are on clearly marked private property. But he can't leave Tom out there alone. He has to call someone. After much consideration and deciding upon the Coastguard as the best bet, he pulls his phone out of his jeans pocket. "Aagh! No reception. How about you?"

Jack immediately grabs for his rucksack and after rustling around inside, pulls out his own mobile and checks it. "Nope. Nothing. What are we going to do?"

"Nine-nine-nine calls are supposed to work even without a signal, aren't they?" Lewis dials as he speaks. It doesn't ring. Either what he had heard was false or something is preventing the emergency call from going through.

Jack also tries, frantically poking the nine button. Still nothing. They all had the sense to fully charge their phones before they left home and having had no reason to use their phones yet, Jack and Lewis still have maximum charge. Lewis reaches for Tom's rucksack and finding his mobile, also indicating a full battery, dials nine-nine-nine. No ring, not even a click. He can't reach emergency services.

Their mood darkens. Tom has still not returned. "Where can he be?" asks Lewis, more to himself than to Jack, not really expecting an answer.

"And what *was* that scratching noise in the first place?" Jack adds, his anxiety rising yet again as he remembers why Tom had left the room. They can't think of where to look or what to do. They know that it is too dangerous to venture out from the cottage, therefore, the only thing they can do, is search for him in the morning as soon as it becomes light. Try as they might, neither can sleep and so that they don't feel they are just ignoring their friend's concerning absence, the silence is soon filled with conversation about Tom.

"Do you remember when we were standing waiting to cross at the zebra crossing and that German shepherd just turned around and nipped him on the chest for no reason?" Lewis recollects.

"Ha, ha! Yes! and remember Emily's horse? When Tom was holding it, so she could run up the path to her friend's house? That suddenly bit him on the chest. Same side too. Horrible big bruise afterwards," Jack replies.

"Must be something funny about Tom's chest." Lewis laughs a little wistfully at the memory of their friend's misfortune, doing nothing but minding his own business or, worse, trying to be helpful.

"Or zebra crossings! Don't forget the little Westie that cocked its leg and weed all over Tom's sock and shoe when we were waiting to cross by the library. That was a zebra crossing again," Jack adds sounding more disheartened than amused. Normally they would have roared with laughter at the recollection of this, but each feels miserable and guilty.

"For such a great guy he has really been quite unfortunate when you think about it," Lewis declares, adding, "Do you know what happened to his foot when his grandad was digging the garden?"

Jack shakes his head.

"Tom was only little and apparently, he had been sitting on the grass alongside his grandad whilst he dug the flower border. Tom buried his foot in the mud and his grandad accidentally stuck the garden fork right into it. Had to go to hospital for that, of course." Lewis cringes at the thought. He can't help feeling subdued and that something unfortunate has happened to Tom yet again. Rather than think of Tom in danger, Lewis tries to turn the conversation to something more cheery remarking, "Probably only fair though I guess as he's the one who's been blessed with all the brains and personality. He can't have it all good. Wouldn't be fair on the rest of us." His mirthless smile gives the game away that despite listing only two of what Lewis considers to be Tom's many attributes, he still sounds and looks downhearted.

"Yeah! and he's got a big house and goes on fabulous holidays." Jack tries to also put a positive spin on the more material plus points, but it only heightens the fact that Tom has gone missing, and they feel totally and utterly helpless.

"We should have gone with him," Lewis adds feeling dejected.

"Yeah. At least one of us should have gone," Jack murmurs in low spirits, knowing that it should have been him and quietly wriggling his way further down into his sleeping bag.

Having heard all this going on, Tom waits patiently outside until everything is quiet. He's been waiting ages and thought they would never settle. The night is emphasising the drop in the early autumn temperature, and he shudders.

When Tom is satisfied that all is calm inside the cottage, he stands on a large lumpy boulder so that he can reach the windowless hole to the Ouija room and leans in, tilts his head backwards and shines his torch up under his chin. The light makes his face appear frighteningly white in the darkness with cavernous dark holes for his mouth and eyes. "Mwahahahaha!" he lets out a deep, maniacal laugh, trying to sound like his idea of the Devil.

Lewis and Jack both scream, pulling their sleeping bags tightly over their heads. Jack is no more than a lump inside quilted material and the only evidence of Lewis's existence is the fringe of ginger tendrils curling their way over the sleeping bag like orange fingers.

Despite trying his best not to, Tom sniggers then completely cracks up into loud guffaws. 'That'll teach them to leave me to go off searching on my own,' he thinks, his sides hurting with the pain of his belly laugh.

It is only when Lewis recognises the sound of Tom's laugh, that he bursts out of his sleeping bag, cursing Tom. "You absolute *#+¥€%#*."

Jack is much slower to emerge, with only his eyes peeking out. He wants to be absolutely sure it really is only Tom, and not some monstrous, evil demon before he feels safe enough to reappear.

Tom returns inside and Lewis, initially furious at Tom for having made him so scared, can't help but be relieved that he is safe. He also accepts that he and Jack deserve everything they get and therefore forgives Tom almost immediately. Jack doesn't need to excuse Tom's trick. He isn't even angry. He's just absolutely delighted that it really was only Tom and not the Devil.

The three initially chuckle when they hear how Tom had thought he was going to die when faced with two dark, staring eyes, but that the scratching sound had turned out to be a sheep rubbing itself on the doorframe. But when he elaborates on how the fear had meant he nearly stopped breathing, Jack's face shows that it has brought home to him just how scary this place is and he no longer sees the funny side.

"Look, I really don't think this is such a good idea after all," he suggests, despite there being an explanation for both the earlier noise in the cottage and the scary face at the window.

Lewis, remembering how anxious he has felt numerous times this evening already, agrees. "Yeah, maybe we've spent enough time here. We said we'd visit at night, and we've done it so perhaps we should go now."

"Sorry, guys, it's way too dangerous to go back down at this time of night! Trust me. I've been out there for ages. I know! It's pitch black and the ground is unstable because of the loose rocks." Remembering his own quandary earlier he adds, "But hey, fam, we actually agreed *all* night not just *at* night, yeah? So let's stick with it, eh?" Tom looks questioningly at Jack and Lewis seeking their approval and the other two, not wanting to look like cowards, merely nod, albeit in

Jack's case, very unconvincingly. "We are all cool, yeah?" Tom looks from Lewis to Jack and holds his clenched fist out towards them, waiting. Lewis looks sheepish, but trying to disguise his anxiety, and always trusting in Tom, he fist-bumps him to indicate that he is okay with the idea of staying. Jack has no option but to appear cool and do likewise.

"Right then, dudes, enough excitement for one evening, time to sleep!" asserts Tom.

Getting into their sleeping bags, Lewis winks at Jack and watches Tom intently.

Tom's leg touches something large, hairy and hard. He yells. "Aaagh! what the actual…" Scrabbling back out as quickly as he can his heart is doing somersaults in his chest, and he looks like he is running on the spot as he cries, "Aagh! Aagh! There's a head in my bag, dudes, a head!"

The other two start laughing as Lewis reaches over into Tom's sleeping bag and pulls out the grey polystyrene head and neck-shaped wig stand complete with long, wavy brown wig he'd put in there when Tom was outside. Holding the wig out in one hand and a smooth, life size head and face with indentations for eyes and the sculpted outline of lips and a nose in the other, Lewis tries to show Tom it had just been a prank. He'd been waiting for an opportunity to freak one of his mates out and after Tom frightening them at the window, it seemed the perfect time and opportunity to do so.

Seeing the funny side, Tom joins in with the laughing and punches Lewis repeatedly on the arm "You total ass. Where the heck did you get that?"

"Owww, that hurts. I brought it from home. It's my nan's," Lewis replies, still laughing as he takes the playful battering from Tom.

With a perfectly reasonable explanation for everything that has happened so far, the three finally relax, and feeling tired after all the excitement, they turn off their torches and lanterns and eventually two of them doze off to sleep.

Tom, however, doesn't. He lays there churning over all the events of the day in his mind. The beauty of the landscape as they sat and ate on the way up; the barbed wire fence surrounding the property; the far more serious injury that could have befallen Lewis when he fell down the hole; beers with the bikers; and then of course, there was the sheep. He smiles to himself wryly, shaking his head in the dark. That flaming sheep. He really thought he was going to be a goner at that point.

Chapter Nine

Lewis is breathing heavily. Surely, he's not going to have another asthma attack this soon after the other? Lewis starts mumbling, and quickly realising that he is dreaming, Tom again grins in the dark and listens to see if Lewis comes out with anything that he can tease him about in the morning. The dream is obviously getting more detailed, as the crinkling of the nylon sleeping bag moving on the stone floor indicates Lewis must be twitching. Tom switches on his torch. He'd better check him.

Lewis doesn't wake up. The light doesn't even break through into his dream. In fact, Lewis starts writhing violently and shaking his head, then his back leaves the floor as his chest pushes towards the ceiling. The mumbling is getting louder and turns to groans. Lewis sounds like he is chanting something. Then he slaps the hard floor with his one good hand and swiftly sits bolt upright, his mouth wide open as though he is screaming but no sound is coming out. Lewis's expression quickly changes from one of shock to grief as tears stream from his eyes, dropping to form small dark patches on his sleeping bag.

Jack, too, jumps into a sitting position looking shocked.

Tom holds his hand up towards Jack as though to stop him from speaking as he addresses Lewis. "It's okay, mate, it's only a dream. You've had a bad dream."

Momentarily Lewis doesn't know where he is and looks around the room as though he hasn't seen it before. His breathing slows as gradually he remembers the cottage and why he is there. Tom's words have calmed him but quickly his eyes seek out Jack. It's okay. Lewis lets his shoulders and his whole body, sag. Jack is fine. All of them are fine.

He doesn't feel the need to say anything. What could he say? So, Lewis simply wipes his eyes with the back of his sleeve and wriggles back into his sleeping bag. Raising his eyebrows, Jack looks at Tom quizzically and is met with a shrug. Tom lays back down and Jack, realising no discussion is forthcoming, does the same.

To say that Lewis still feels unsettled would be an understatement. The dream had been so real. He can still see everything so clearly. He can hear the repetitive voice and smell the rich, perfumed aroma that still clings to the insides of his nostrils. Lewis thinks of the man he had seen in a black hooded cloak, his back turned towards him as he faced a sort of altar. But was he a man or was he some sort of beast? It sounded like a man's voice. It was deep and he had been quietly chanting something over and over, but Lewis couldn't hear most of the words, just something about 'great master, mystical spirit, I give to thee'. The earthy, woody smell was coming from small black cones that were sending dark slithers of smoke upwards. Lewis could see a black velvet cloth covering the altar on which, positioned to the right, was a black orb shaped crystal perched on a black three-legged stand. The orb was so smooth and shiny that it reflected the image of the room like a mirror and although he couldn't see clearly, it hinted at the side of a man's face. Suddenly the face had changed to blood red, with a long dark beard and cold orange eyes with horizontal slits. Momentarily it had stared back at him before again returning to the profile of an unknown man.

Next to the orb there had been a wooden bowl piled high with what looked like dried leaves or perhaps herbs and in the centre of the altar, a big black book, ornately decorated around the edges with a dull metal, like pewter. The raised metal skull on the front had what looked like a real eyeball staring out from one socket. To the left-hand side of the altar was a glass jar filled with small shards of glass and metal nails. There were two black candles, one in the shape of a nude female and one, alight, the wick flickering, in the shape of a nude male.

Lewis feels giddy as the shadow of a body laying still, further back on the altar, comes crawling back into his mind, wavers and disappears again like mist. There is something familiar about the memory of the shadowy being. He closes his eyes and again the hazy figure is still atop the black velvet cloth. Lewis blinks repeatedly as he tries to bring the picture into clearer focus. The cloaked man raises something clutched between his two hands above his head and points it towards the shadow. It looks like the hilt of a dagger. His voice louder now, he calls out, "Hunter, master of the black arts…"

The shadow turns its face towards him. It's Jack. Jack is nothing but a dusky silhouette laying on the altar, but his eyes are clear and piercing and they are looking plaintively straight into Lewis's own. Silently begging, pleading for Lewis to help him. Lewis feels faint. He's awake and he has just seen Jack sitting up, also clearly awake and unharmed but he cannot shake the heavy nauseous feeling in his stomach that this had been more than a dream. Worse than a nightmare even.

Chapter Ten

At some time during what is left of the night they are suddenly and very harshly awakened.

Bang bang bang. Their hearts are audibly pounding in the otherwise silent cottage. The three simultaneously jump to a sitting position.

"Oh God, oh God, no!" pleads Jack, gripping his sleeping bag to his chest.

"Get a freaking grip, bro." Tom is now beyond frustrated with Jack's repeated panicking. It is putting everyone on edge. He has already worked out what the noise is. "It's only what's left of the wooden shutter banging on the window. Look!" Holding up his lantern, two horizontal pieces of wood, hanging by a sliver of dull metal, clearly demonstrate Tom's explanation as the wind blows and they hit the wall. "Your turn this time, Jacko, go and tie it back or knock it off or something so it doesn't keep us all awake."

Looking shocked at Tom's suggestion that he should go, Jack stammers, "B-b-b-b-but that means I'll have to go outside."

"Well Lewis can hardly do it with only one arm, and I've already been, so just go!" Tom asserts, pointing. He is thinking that off the waves or the skate park Jack really is *not* cool.

Muttering his complaints about going and not wanting to leave the safety of his sleeping-bag, Jack hops like an upright caterpillar out of the room. They hear him bouncing and thudding his way over the wooden floorboards through the cottage.

Bang bang bang. Jack has been gone for over five minutes, but the window shutter is still knocking against the stone wall.

"Get on with it, Jack," Tom calls from inside. The shutter continues, *bang bang bang.* "What on earth are you doing out there. Just hit the darn thing off," Tom yells, getting impatient. He is tired and really wants to sleep. The shutter continues thumping against the building and still there is no reply from Jack.

Lewis's eyes burst open and lifting his head, he cocks it to one side to listen. He thinks he hears a deep grunt. A snort, like an angry bull. There is a loud jarring, grating sound. Something is scrabbling on the ground outside causing the loose rocks to tumble. Then a terrifying scream.

"Let me go, please, please, let me go," Jack is shrieking. A dull thud follows, then another, then another, and then nothing but a deathly silence.

Lewis looks horrified but Tom is more cynical, and thinking Jack is just trying to repay him for messing about outside the window earlier calls out, "Yeah, yeah, done it, read the book, worn the T-shirt. Maybe pick a different window to prat about in, eh? Jerk!" Tom is irritated at Jack's apparent lack of originality.

Jack trying to scare them hadn't crossed Lewis's mind until that point but now realising what the noises outside were, he echoes Tom's comment, "Yeah, total jerk," and shuffles lopsidedly back into his sleeping bag. Seizing his opportunity, Lewis pulls his rucksack to him and feels around for something he had hidden in there, then reaching out towards Tom who remains sitting, waiting for Jack to return, says, "I um, I made you this" He hands Tom a small wooden cross hanging on a black twisted thread. "Didn't know what might be up here. Crosses are supposed to protect you against vampires and that sort of thing."

Tom, not quite knowing what to say or how to react, looks at Lewis who awkwardly adds, "You know, just in case like." Lewis is now feeling a mixture of embarrassment and stupidity, but before he had realised it was only Jack mucking about outside, the noise had made him think that this was the perfect time to give Tom the gift.

"Wow! That's really kind. Clever! Thank you," Tom replies, thinking that crosses are not really his thing and that it feels like a bit of an overkill to be protecting him against ghouls. Nevertheless, he thinks it was nice of Lewis to have gone to the trouble of making it so he immediately, and very politely, slips it over his head.

"What… are you doing… in… *my* house?" a deep throaty voice, sinister in its quietness, hisses. Lewis and Tom snap their heads around to look at each other. "Get out! Leave my house *now*!" There is no mistaking that the menacing voice sounds threatening, and it really doesn't sound like Jack. The banging has stopped, and an eerie silence follows until Tom catches his breath. Peering through the black hole is a huge, demonic, crimson red face, with long black hair hanging from its chin and horns spiralling to a point from the top of its head. Piercing gold eyes with wide, horizontal black slits for irises are staring straight at him. The thing is breathing heavily, snorting two streams of visible vapour into the room.

Tom's blood runs cold; this very definitely isn't Jack. His heart is racing so hard he can't get enough oxygen to speak. "L-l-l-l-lewis, I think we've got trouble. Big, big trouble," he says, then more urgently, "*Lewis!*"

Lewis has already scrambled out of his bag and is backed up against the wall, rigid with fear. Having to force himself to move, Tom places his hands behind him and walks backwards like a crab, very slowly and very quietly inching his way out of his own sleeping bag and up against the wall alongside Lewis. The red face stares at them, its golden eyes not blinking, burrowing deep into theirs, hot steam curling from each nostril.

"What do we do?" Lewis pleads in a whisper, clenching his fists so tightly that his nails dig painfully into his palms.

"If we stay, we're trapped and if we go out, we're done for," Tom concedes, sweat now trickling down the back of his neck and between his shoulder blades. Pressing their backs even harder against the wall as though they hoped it would swallow them up, the two are totally helpless. Tom tries to think quickly. His breath catching, he suggests, "K-k-kitchen. Back door. Sheep. Cupboard." He nods to his left.

Not completely understanding what Tom means, but at least understanding that they were headed for the kitchen or the back door, Lewis follows as Tom, his eyes firmly fixed on the horrifying face snorting through the window, slowly shuffles along the wall little by little towards the narrow doorway.

Outside the snorting has now reached the pitch of raging bellows. They hear what sounds like hundreds of stones being thrown in different directions as something clatters and thunders hooves on the rocks. Reaching what had once been some sort of kitchen but not wanting to go outside, Tom grabs the black metal latch on a long, old, wooden door. He pulls and pulls,,but having probably not been opened for a very long time, it just won't budge. He wriggles his fingers down the gap at the side and grapples with it. Eventually, creaking its objection, it gives a little, opening slightly. Lewis joins in with his one good arm and together they manage to drag the door towards them and hurriedly enter a very, very small room, immediately wrestling the door closed behind them again.

It appears to be more like a large cupboard, similar to the pantry Lewis has at the farmhouse, but there's no lock.

Clip clip clip clip. It sounds like hooves on a stone floor. The thing is inside. Tom and Lewis freeze, holding their breath. The sound stops. It is in the kitchen. *Clip clip.* It isn't moving away. It knows they are here, and it must be turning in circles, looking for them. 'What the hell is it?' thinks Tom. What kind of monstrous demon had they just seen? Tom feels light-headed as he holds his breath. *Clip clip clip clip.* They hear it treading across the rough stone kitchen floor into the next room and on through the cottage. Sometimes it sounds like it is moving further away and at other times, coming closer again. It is searching, backwards and forwards, backwards and forwards. Tom feels sick to the pit of his stomach as he realises that in their hurry to hide, they have totally trapped themselves. If the *thing* finds them, they are in a closed cupboard with no window, and therefore, other than the door leading straight into the *thing's* path, no possible way out. *Clip, clip.* They hear it coming back towards the kitchen. *Clip, clip, clip, clip.* It's getting closer… and closer… and closer.

What chance have they got? Tom shuts his eyes. The *thing* snorts loudly again. As though it is sniffing out prey, it takes a deep breath in and sharply exhales it out, like a dog when it smells perfume or something it finds unpleasant or overpowering. Vapour is creeping under the door, through the cracks and down the sides of the doorframe like a moist, warm fog. Both Tom and Lewis are only too well aware of just how close it must now be, as a strong, musty smell reaches their nostrils. Despite every inch of his body telling him otherwise, Tom still hopes, just for a split second, that it is the sheep again, but his gut is telling him equally quickly that it is just wishful thinking. The smell is so pungent that despite his fear, Tom cannot help but screw up his face, and opening his eyes he looks at Lewis who can only offer an almost imperceptible nod. Tom takes it as an implication that he has also smelled it.

However, Lewis had intended the nod to infer that not only could he smell it but that he recognised it. 'Urine-soaked hay,' thinks Lewis, familiar with the odour from cleaning out the livestock at home. He feels a strong urge to actually see the thing. He has to know what it is, what is going to put an end to his too short life. Without moving his feet, he leans forward and squinting one eye closed, he puts the other to the vapour laced crack in the wood panel of the door. Lewis is incredulous. If his own eyes weren't gazing directly upon it, he would not have believed what he can see. A huge, long-haired black goat, taller than a man, and far too tall for the height of the tiny kitchen, is standing on its back legs also leaning forward with its disproportionately large head hunched into its shoulders. Its bearded face looks red raw and sore, 'Like burned or peeled skin,' thinks Lewis.

A picture that he had once seen of the Devil depicted as a goat, leaps into Lewis's mind. The *thing* is not just a *thing*, it's a *beast*, a demonic looking *beast*. The very *beast* he had seen mirrored in the orb in his dream. It hadn't been a man at all. 'Or was it both?' the thought momentarily flashes in front of Lewis.

"Come now, where… are you?" It has its head cocked to one side, almost leaning on its own shoulder. "There's a way out of this you know. A way to an everlasting world if, *if,*" it emphasised the last word before continuing, "you are willing to give your life for the black arts. *If…* you are willing to give your life to me." Its ears flick backwards and forwards as it appears to listen, waiting for their response. Its leering eyes, full of evil intent would be looking straight into Lewis's had the wooden door not been between them, making Lewis instantly feel the need to avoid its gaze and look down to the floor even though, as far as he is aware, it can't see him.

The *beast* is very still and no longer snorting but both Tom and Lewis can hear it breathing. It must know they are here. They both close their eyes, hold their breath, and wait for the inevitable horror that is bound to befall them. The latch clicks. Tom puts his hand across his mouth. He is going to be sick. The latch clicks again and again and eventually the door creaks but does not open. Again, *click, creak, click, click, creak*. They know they are done for; they know they are going to die. It is now only a matter of time. So, like captured prey, petrified, they hold their breath and simply await their awful but inevitable fate.

Chapter Eleven

Just as the lack of oxygen is making them feel giddy and they desperately need to take a deep breath, they realise that the *beast* is no longer trying the door. *Clip clip clip clip*. Is it really possible that it couldn't open the door and it's walking away? Lewis stops himself from sighing with relief as he realises it really is actually leaving! Why didn't it just yank the door off? he thinks, it certainly looked strong enough. It can't have believed they were in there. 'Probably thought that if it couldn't pull the door open, we wouldn't be able to,' Lewis very quickly surmises. But neither he nor Tom dare move; they have to hold on longer until they are absolutely sure it's leaving.

Clip, clip, clip, clip. The sound is getting fainter and faster. Tom and Lewis can't hold their breath any longer and with their heads thrown back they simultaneously gasp oxygen into their lungs. Then once again, other than their eyes fixed on each other, they stand, muscles tensed and wait. *Has it gone, has it really gone? Where is Jack? What should they do now? Should they run or is it waiting for them to show themselves and catch them outside?* All these questions and many more are racing through Tom and Lewis's minds. But without even speaking a word to each other they both instinctively know that the very best thing to do is to do *nothing*; just wait, and wait, and wait.

Lewis gasps for breath again, then again, and again. Hearing this new burst of sudden intakes of breath, Tom automatically assumes it must be in response to the *beast* returning. He inwardly panics, his stomach lurching, and bile rises up into his mouth. He listens carefully. No snorting or hooves. Even the acrid smell has finally disappeared. In fact, not only can't he hear anything untoward, it is eerily quiet. The only sound is that of whistling and that's in the cupboard with him. Lewis looks clammy and is now wheezing. 'Oh no, he's having another asthma attack.' He gestures to Lewis, holding an imaginary inhaler in his hand and miming someone taking a puff on it. Lewis looks dejected and shakes his head. Tom realises he's left his inhaler in his rucksack or sleeping bag and they are both back in the Ouija room.

Tom is in a turmoil. He can't risk coming out of the cupboard in case the *beast* is out there, silently waiting. It may hear him forcing open the ill-fitting old door as it grazes loudly across the floorboards and then it will come back and kill them. He looks at Lewis helplessly. His nostrils are flaring, open and closed, open and closed. He can see that he can't expand his chest enough to get a proper breath and is trying hard not to cough, but all Tom can do is look at him weakly. Lewis's lips are beginning to turn slightly blue as he slides, slowly, down the wall, and slumping he falls into unconsciousness, half sitting, half laying on the cold floor. A confusing mixture of feelings immediately engulf Tom. He is completely torn. If he leaves the current safety of the cupboard, he doesn't know what horror could happen if the *beast* catches them, but feeling wretched knows that without his inhaler, Lewis could die. The hopelessness of his dilemma weighing heavily on him, Tom sits down next to Lewis. His emotions too much to bear, he too falls into the blissful nothingness of darkness.

Waking again only a very short while later, Tom can see the slightest glimmer of light coming through gaps in the side of the door, landing on the far wall as though someone had scrubbed little patches of the stone with bleach. He doesn't know if he too had fainted, his body shut down through fear, or whether he had merely fallen asleep due to sheer exhaustion. Almost scared to look, afraid of what he may find, he quickly turns his head to check on Lewis leaning, sling-side, against him. "Lewis. Lewis." No response. He props him back up, but he doesn't stir. Tom is almost overjoyed when he hears Lewis quietly rasping. He is at least breathing. Tom knows that he now has no option but to go and get help. Quickly!

Manoeuvring Lewis away from the doorway and leaning him against the wall, Tom pulls and pulls on the old wooden door knowing from last night that with enough effort it will eventually give way. The rough edge at the bottom snags and cracks across the stone floor until he successfully forces it open. Tom stands there and once again, he waits. Has the noise alerted the *beast* and will it now come back? If it's still around it will undoubtedly have heard him opening the door. Through the doorless kitchen, Tom sees that daylight is just breaking through. With his heart thudding in his chest and his ears pricked, alert to any sound, he gingerly walks through to the Ouija room and checks in Lewis's rucksack. No inhaler. He partially unzips his sleeping bag and feels around inside. Nothing!

"I can't believe this. What else can go wrong? Where the bloody hell have you put it, Lewis?" he says out loud, not usually given to swearing but now frustratedly shaking the sleeping bag. He grabs his own rucksack, leaving the rest of their belongings on the floor, and is just about to walk out of the room when the increasing light through the windowless hole in the wall reflects on something out of the corner of his eye. "Yes, thank you. Thank you!" He walks back and picks up the inhaler from against the wall. Lewis must have dropped it there when he moved his sleeping bag forward, away from the mould, or knocked it back there when he frantically wriggled backwards out of it.

"Lewis. I've got your inhaler. Here." Lewis doesn't open his eyes. His shallow rasping breath continues. "Lewis, buddy, please. You need to wake up and use your inhaler." Tom waves it around in front of Lewis's face and even tries to force it into his hands but he may as well have been offering it to an alien with no eyes who doesn't speak English. Tom holds the inhaler against Lewis's lips and presses down, hoping that Lewis will instinctively place his mouth around it and breathe in, but he doesn't. Using his forefinger, Tom presses down once more but Lewis fails to respond. Tom knows that Lewis needs more help now than an inhaler is going to provide. "I won't be long, mate. I'm going to get help."

Throwing his rucksack over his shoulder he walks through the cottage and stands in the doorway. It looks and feels peaceful outside. There is no hint of the horrors of the previous night. The sun, although not visible itself on the horizon, is showing its presence by casting a hazy light up into the sky. The air has a chill to it and the bushes are covered with dewy spiders' webs that always remind Tom of this time of year. His Aunt Stella calls it a 'back to school kind of day'.

Tom turns to his right out of the door and picks his way across the rubble, heading away from the cottage. His return down the hill is a difficult one. He daren't run as he still can't see in the dim light but knows he can't afford to waste any time. Many times, he stumbles over rocks, or slips on the wet moss or damp, boggy mud. "Please be okay, Lewis, please," he repeatedly chants as he quickens his pace only to fall yet again. He knows he may still have a chance of saving Lewis if, and it's a big if, he can get down off the moor without meeting the *beast*.

Tom tries desperately not to even think about Jack. 'Is he safe? Where is he? Is he laying injured or frightened somewhere?' He dared not allow the thought that Jack may already be dead enter his mind. He can only concentrate on the things he can do something about and right now that, he figures, is getting help for Lewis. His legs and arms are scratched and the wet ground, finding a way to soak through the tiny holes surrounding the fastenings of his walking boots, is making his socks and feet cold and wet but staring at the undulating ground below him, he continues on and on.

Tom feels like he has been walking for hours and stops to assess how far he has yet to go. Looking up, he sees daylight has overtaken the darkness of night. He shakes his head, puzzled, then his throat tightens and completely deflated and dejected he drops to his knees. Only fifty or so metres away, directly facing him, is the cottage, its glassless windows staring at him sarcastically. It is laughing at him. He's been walking round and round in circles all this time and he is right back where he started. Brave, calm Tom is in a turmoil and tears build in his eyes, falling unashamedly as the hopelessness of his situation hits him. He grasps his hair with both hands. Does he spend hours walking in search of help again only to risk coming back to the same starting point? Mr Marchant was right about the moor. No wonder people got lost and died here. He hates it. He hates its greenery. He hates its purple heather and yellow gorse. He hates its ugly grey rocks and most of all he hates the cottage. He hates that more than he has ever hated anything in his life.

***

Lewis is as Tom had left him, in a sitting position, slumped against the wall. His breathing is now even more laboured and shallow. Tom's decision is made. He has to stay; it's too risky to leave Lewis now. He could stop breathing at any time. At least he can perform CPR and breathe for him if he needs to. Crestfallen, Tom slumps down on the hard floor facing Lewis, watches him and listens to his breath. His only hope is that Jack has made it home or that some other foolhardy idiot decides to visit the cottage soon.

Chapter Twelve

Tom thinks that the lonely coffin is perfect for Jack, if, he reflects, you can ever call a coffin perfect. The sides depict turquoise waters and a surfer riding a cresting wave that curls over the lid to meet a clear blue summer's sky. On top, a small circular wreath of silver white flowers, sit like the sun amongst the expanse of cloudless, soft blue. Close by, pale-faced and feeling numb, Tom and Lewis sit in the second pew at the front of the church; one smart shiny dark-haired head and one with a neatly trimmed crop of ginger curls, bowed, as the vicar reads Jack's eulogy. Their new, dark suits, white shirts and black ties give their already pallid skin a sickly hue. The pew in front is empty, as is the one behind. Their parents, two rows further back, are not only not allowed to sit with them but are not permitted to be in physical reach of them. Instead of having the support from their families, Tom and Lewis are each flanked by a uniformed officer. Nevertheless, they have to be grateful that at least Jack's mum, Mrs Dory, had believed them and had even gone so far as eventually managing to persuade the reluctant police and local authority that, until proven guilty, they should be presumed innocent and as such their presence should be permitted at the funeral of their friend.

Tom and Lewis had been found in a closed pantry in the ruins of the derelict cottage by a young couple. Like many others before them, and no doubt many after, they had come early the following afternoon to explore the home of the Satanic worshipper and no doubt write their names on the cottage walls to demonstrate they too were brave enough to have entered.

Lewis had been going in and out of consciousness and Tom, reluctant to leave him, had been sitting for so long he had dead legs and had been unable to get up even when he had heard movement outside. If it had been the demonic *beast* returning, he would have had to offer himself up as fair game. Having no mobile signal to call for help, the girl had remained with them, more by way of support to the usually well balanced and realistic Tom who had then appeared completely helpless and forlorn. Her boyfriend had gone hot foot back down the craggy hillside, meeting the Coastguard who, as luck would have it, were already on their way up. They had been alerted by the police when Lewis's parents had reported that their son had failed to return that morning. Both Tom and Lewis had been hospitalised, "Just to be on the safe side," the doctor had said. Tom and Lewis could only hope that Jack had done what he had threatened earlier the night before and had gone home. Tom was subsequently released late that same evening and Lewis, due to his need for a nebuliser, ongoing monitoring of his breathing and an X-ray of his wrist, was not released until the following day.

Tom and Lewis's release was short-lived. Whilst they were being checked over in hospital, search and rescue dogs had tracked their friend, Jack, from the sleeping bag they found outside the cottage, beneath the window. The bag was almost unidentifiable, the covering now no more than frazzled shreds, attached by sinewy threads of stiff cotton or long, individual strips of frayed and lacerated material waving in the wind from where they had been hooked by the thorny gorse; the white stuffing filler streaming out and covering the surrounding moss-covered rocks and bushes like patches of soft, un-melted snow. The sleeping bag, ground and cottage walls couldn't just be described as splattered in blood; they were drenched in it.

Without exception, none of the rescue team had ever attended such a macabre find. Many felt nauseous and some were sick to their boots. But they hadn't known whether this was as a result of the sheer volume of blood or the weird, fetid smell of stale urine that the whole area seemed to have been dowsed in. The dogs, however, had thankfully had no such reaction. They had their job to do, and following the scent trail from the gruesome scene at the cottage, they tracked it back to Jack's lifeless, broken body where it lay in a grave of sharp gorse and heather at the bottom of the craggy, granite rocks, hundreds of feet below.

Tom and Lewis, being the last people to have seen Jack alive, were interviewed as potential witnesses but soon found themselves in police custody, suspected of Jack's murder. Admittedly Jack had irritated them both; more on this trip than in all the years they had known each other. Not only hadn't he been in the least bit cool, he had actually turned out to be a total wimp, they had agreed, but when all was said and done, he had still been their friend and they were going to miss him desperately. Why would they want to murder him? No one would murder someone for being scared, no one. Therefore, other than the overwhelming sadness at the tragic loss of their friend, Tom firmly believed that they had nothing to worry about. After all, they too had nearly been victims themselves.

It had soon become clear, however, that no one believed them; not the social services or even the legal representatives their parents had called in, never mind the actual detectives interviewing them. To be fair, even Tom and Lewis could both understand how far-fetched and ridiculous their story of a goat-like Devil sounded. But what made it worse, far, far worse, was that the detectives said they had evidence that they had injured Jack. Actual, tangible *evidence*. Traces of Jack's blood had been found under Tom's nails, and despite his protestations and explanation that he had cleaned up a wound on Jack's shoulder when he had backed into the doorway and caught a nail, they clearly didn't believe him. They even tried to offer up the tear in his rucksack, from when he had been caught by the barbed wire fence, as having been caused by a struggle. The detectives went on to claim they had further proof. Proof that the tears and mud all over Lewis's jumper, along with the scratches on his back and arms, were likely to have been caused by Jack fighting back. This was, they alleged, further backed up by Lewis's blood traces being found within the creases of Jack's own fingers. Significant indications that he had been trying to defend himself, they said.

Of course there would be mud stains and scratches, Tom had argued, and of course there would be blood. Jack had helped pull Lewis to safety after he had taken that nasty fall in the grounds. Both he and Lewis had even shown the police precisely where the fall had happened, when they had been taken, under escort, back up to the cottage. The corrugated roofing was still wallowing on its side in the hole and even the hospital had confirmed that Lewis had sustained a sprained wrist. As a result of a defensive struggle, the police contended.

So here they are, not only standing before their friend's coffin, which Tom thinks is painful and wretched enough, but remanded in custody accused of his murder. They are living a nightmare. A nightmare that could, potentially, have very horrible, long-standing consequences.

What hurts Tom nearly as much as losing his friend and not being believed, however, is the additional, unbearable hell that he knows Lewis is going through. Lewis keeps seeing the thing, the *beast*, everywhere; convinced that it is still coming for him. Tom could hear him screaming along the corridor at night as he dreamed of the *beast* snorting and pawing the ground before it opened the cupboard door and attacked him, ripping the skin from his small, light-skinned body. These weren't just nightmares. Tom heard him banging on the door, pleading, even when he was awake, tormented by the vapour that he was adamant was coming out of a tap, under the door or through the tiniest crack in the window frame or plasterwork on the wall. Poor Lewis was filled with dread at even just having to go to the bathroom, in case there was the faintest smell of urine. Something he could not, for obvious reasons, avoid doing.

Lewis had always been the happy go lucky, positive thinking optimist of the three and now Tom can hardly recognise him. He is receiving counselling for post-traumatic stress disorder. A guilt reaction to the atrocities he had inflicted upon Jack, they had implied. Tom questions whether Lewis will ever again be the person he used to be. He had always been aware that he had a special place in Lewis's heart and that Lewis had high expectations of him but there is nothing he can do or say to make his friend feel better. Nothing!

Fingering the handmade cross around his neck, Tom starts to wonder if it had been responsible for supporting him in some way. Had the thought, effort and affection that Lewis had put into whittling it, given it some protective quality? After all, other than the dire legal situation they are in — and Tom is confident that their innocence will soon be recognised — it suddenly hits him that he is the only one of the three left relatively unscathed. Other than its face at the window, he hadn't actually seen the *beast*, like Lewis had, so he couldn't really picture it or have his dreams filled with its image like Lewis did. He wasn't still imagining its presence or reacting to every unusual sound like Lewis. Neither was he dead like Jack! And he didn't even want to let his mind think about what tormenting fear and agonising pain poor Jack must have suffered. So had the cross protected him or had his grandfather, GBM, George Bartholomew Milton had a hand in keeping him safe? Something or someone had!

***

Tom and Lewis's respective parents, clothed in traditional mourning black, are sitting side by side, gazing at the back of the boys' heads. They know their boys and unconditionally believe in their innocence. Nevertheless, in addition to feeling desperately sad at the death of Jack and horror at how it came about, both sets of parents feel tremendous guilt at having let their young sons go on such an adventure. They have become unlikely but firm friends, having found comfort in each other's company. Reassuring each other that they hadn't been wrong to let them go. That Tom and Lewis were growing up. That they had needed to experience life. That they had taken every precaution.

Jack's mother, however, refusing to conform to the standard expectation of black attire, is sporting what can only be described as colourful, boho chic harem pants, gathered with elastic at the ankle; beaded espadrilles and a pale blue vintage geometric design, tassel-bottomed top. She is sitting alone in the front pew on the other side of the aisle, dabbing her eyes and blowing her nose into the same scrunched up bunch of now off-white, damp tissues.

Jack's estranged father has even shown up and taken the pew behind her. He has tried to look formal, but his suit is ill-fitting. The jacket is a different material and therefore different shade of black to the trousers and the button up shirt collar is too big for him, causing his black clip-on tie to stick out at a funny angle. Studying him, Tom can't see any resemblance of Jack at all. What he can see, however, is that the poor man looks vacant and totally hopeless, as though he is still undecided as to whether he should even be there or not.

Amelie, wracked with sobs, her eyes red and sore and her nose streaming, is sitting with her parents a few rows behind Mrs Dory, her mother clutching her daughter to her and stroking the top of her head. Tom hasn't heard a word from Mia since she handed him the book the day before he left to go up onto the moor. His eyes search for her. He was hoping for a smile or even just a nod that shows she believes in him and understands the misery of what he is going through, but he won't receive either, as he can't see her anywhere in the congregation. She hasn't come and neither have her parents. Visibly slumping his shoulders, he guesses that she has obviously, and to his mind, understandably, given up on him already.

Tom isn't really listening to the vicar. He can hear his words, but they seem to be washing over him. What he can now hear however is a familiar rumble in the distance that is getting louder and louder until it turns into a clamouring explosion outside, then abruptly stops. Motorcycles! The vicar — who has already had to raise his eyebrows and look sternly out onto some members of the congregation a number of times for whispering in not so hushed tones whilst openly staring at Tom and Lewis — becomes silent, his eyes fixed on the door at the back of the church. Tom and Lewis look at each other, then over their shoulders, as they hear the clump, clump, clump of heavy boots.

Eight leather-jacketed bikers, led by spiderweb man, each clutching helmets respectfully under their arms, have entered through the stone archway. They don't attempt to take one of the many empty pews left at the rear, but line-up, placing their helmets quietly on the floor, then stand, hands folded in front of them, backs against the wood-panelling and heads bowed. Spiderweb man then thuds straight up the aisle. Reaching Jack's coffin, he lays a wreath of blue, white and yellow flowers on the top. Pinned to it a card depicts a helmetless rider, blond surf hair blowing in the breeze astride a chopped motorcycle, joyfully holding a can of beer in the air. Then he simply bows his head and thuds his way back down the aisle watched by the staring, many unashamedly open-mouthed, mourners.

'Wow! They remember Jack, even though he hadn't exactly done much to endear himself to them.' Tom is grateful, further thinking, 'And they have obviously gone to a lot of trouble to have that card made. It perfectly captures their short meeting in the cottage.' Tom has a clear memory of the can of beer incident and is seriously impressed that they are paying tribute to their friend in such a personal and fitting way, albeit a little tongue in cheek, which seems appropriate in the circumstances.

Tom blinks repeatedly as his attention is suddenly and very harshly pulled back to the present. Mrs Dory, the closest to the coffin, has heard a rasping sound coming from inside. She runs to it and soon the rasp turns to louder and more insistent scratching. Believing there has been a terrible mistake, her half smiling, confused expression shows that she is torn between the delight and expectation that her baby, her only baby is, after all, alive and coming back to her, and panic-stricken horror that he is trapped inside a wooden, airless box. "Open it. Quick! Open it, he'll suffocate," she cries, forgetting that he has been dead three weeks now. Clawing at it, she snaps her nails as she struggles to lever off the lid with her bare hands; her face taking on a blotchy purple colour as beads of sweat drip to the floor in her fevered, frenzied effort to release her son. A number of mourners quickly circle the coffin; a fifty-fifty split between those trying to assist Mrs Dory by frantically twitching silver catches or trying to force the top of the casket, and those trying to help by diplomatically assuring Mrs Dory that she is sadly mistaken, and attempting to lead her away.

The vicar decides that the only thing for it is to show Mrs Dory that whatever it is she has heard is not coming from the coffin and that her son is not about to be buried alive. Therefore, in an attempt to retain some composure, he calls for someone to fetch the funeral director waiting outside with the pall bearers.

Tom watches as the funeral director reluctantly starts to loosen the screws. He can't believe what he is seeing and quickly averting his eyes, he wishes that this misery would just end so that he and Lewis could go back to living normal lives. *If* they could ever live a normal life again, that is.

As the lid loosens Lewis sees a wispy stream of moist vapour trailing its way out from under the lid. His mouth starts filling with saliva and his stomach turns as the stench of goat urine reaches his nostrils. Lewis places his hands on top of his head, grabbing handfuls of hair, and starts screaming; a wailing, shrieking scream. Tom turns to look at him. He is rocking backwards and forwards yelling, "Get out! Everyone, get out!" No one seems to be taking any notice even though Lewis knows he's hollering at the top of his voice. "It's the Devil. Get out." Why is no one listening to him? "It will kill you. *All* of you." He is trying to run, his feet paddling just above the floor, but he isn't moving; someone is holding him firmly by the shoulders. He starts thrashing violently but can't get away.

Everyone is now staring at him, looking awkward and embarrassed, as the tears stream down his face. Tom hears the familiar whistle and then the rasp coming from Lewis. Lewis stops fighting and Tom watches him sag, then start checking all his pockets, looking for his inhaler. Lewis is gasping for air.

"Help him, damn you, help him," Tom pleads with the two officers from the young offender Institute, "He's having an asthma attack."

The officer next to Lewis had been trying to restrain him and push him down into his seat. Lewis's sudden let up from resistance has caused him to hit the wooden pew harder than expected and a loud thud, echoes around the vaulted ceiling. Feeling helpless, he tries to reach over to Lewis but the officer next to him pulls him away. Tom can see Lewis deteriorating and shouts at the officers, "Please, he hasn't got his inhaler, he hasn't got his inhaler. He can't breathe." Lewis's breathing is now no more than a hollow rattle. As Tom resists, a firm guiding hand on his elbow steers him out of the pew into the main aisle and towards the back of the church. He looks back over his shoulder at the coffin standing alone in front of the altar. He turns his head to look over his other shoulder at Mrs Dory, her eyes pooled with tears as she looks away from Lewis and gazes at Tom. 'Poor Mrs Dory,' he thinks, 'and poor, poor Lewis. Will his suffering ever end? It's bad enough for both of us waiting for trial for Jack's murder when neither of us have done anything other than survive when Jack hadn't. But his asthma, his nightmares and his hallucinations are just too much for Lewis to bear and too much for me, as a totally helpless friend, to witness!'

All this is flashing through Tom's mind as he notices the eight Bikers looking directly at him, saluting with their right hands. As one their fists clench, and smiling sadly and nodding, they strike their chests then raise their fists into the air. Tom fights the constriction in his throat and the tears that are now threatening to tumble out of his eyes. He not only feels grateful to them on Jack and Mrs Dory's behalf but is now sincerely humbled by their show of solidarity. They obviously believe his innocence.

A lightbulb suddenly switches on in his brain. Of course! Why hadn't he thought of it before? The bikers! Had they heard or seen anything on their short trip onto the moor that ill-fated evening that might vindicate him and Lewis? Have they been interviewed by the police? Had the police even looked for them and if so, how would they know who they even were? Neither he nor Lewis had managed to pick up an actual name for any of them. Surely lots of them with their unusually tattooed faces would be easy to identify, though, especially spiderweb man. But then again, Tom realises, only if they were already known to the police. Were they? He wonders. And would bikers like these even be willing witnesses if they did know something? His mind is racing with questions and possibilities. Tom's heart misses a beat as a spark ignites in his belly and hope starts building within him.

He has been clinging to his enduring belief that the truth will eventually come out; that people will believe that what he and Lewis had said they had experienced *had* really happened; that they had not killed their mate, not even in an accident. They hadn't been 'mucking about or play-fighting' as the solicitor had asked. They hadn't even been real fighting. They both knew in their hearts that Jack hadn't fallen, and they most certainly had not killed him as the police suggested. Somehow, someone, somewhere, would be able to prove it, regardless of how bizarre their account may appear, despite how damning the current evidence and what the police and Crown Prosecution Service believe. Tom cannot think what, but maybe it will be these bikers who throw something into the pot that suggests an alternative explanation and maybe, just maybe, eventually the real but unlikely and horrifying reality of who or what still lives in that hideous cottage on the moor will be realised. After all, Tom's grandfather used to tell him and his sisters, "The truth will always out!"

But who is going to believe that a demonic *beast*, summoned during a Satanic rite by an evil Devil worshipper, still exists in the twenty-first century?

As Tom walks into the low afternoon sun of late autumn, a chilling thought runs cold through his veins. Supposing Lewis's post-traumatic stress hallucinations aren't hallucinations at all. He halts suddenly feeling like a shaft of ice has been stabbed into his chest and out through his back. Supposing Lewis hadn't been dreaming that night in the cottage. Supposing he is psychic and had been given a message. Supposing he had seen what was going to happen and supposing what Lewis is still seeing now is real. Supposing, just supposing, the *beast* has embodied Jack and is now inside that coffin. The coffin that is about to be opened!

Tom's knees buckle, everything goes out of focus and feeling fuzzy, he drops limply to the ground. When he comes round, laying on his back, his face to one side, turned away from the officer leaning over him, the epitaph on an old grey gravestone, slowly comes into focus: 'ABANDON ALL HOPE'.

TO BE CONTINUED